THE CLOWN

Novel

Printed in U.S.A
2026

DAO HIEU

THE CLOWN

Novel

An English translation of the original Vietnamese novel "Thằng Hề" by author Đào Hiếu. Translated by G.Phương Thanh

THE TRAGEDY OF SOUTHERN VIETNAMESE INTELLECTUALS WHO JOINED THE "RESISTANCE AGAINST AMERICA"

NOSTALGIA PUBLISHERS

USA 2026

BEFORE THE STORY

At the end of 1976, I once joined a group of young writers and artists who were invited by Mr. Võ Văn Kiệt, then Secretary of the Ho Chi Minh City Party Committee, to board a small yacht that sailed out to Duyên Hải District (Cần Giờ).

It was in this brackish, saltwater marshland that I met a commune secretary who was about as young as I was at the time. Although I only spoke with him for about an hour, I was truly astonished to realize that I had encountered an *existentialist* - a genuine one - bare and solitary like a lone bush in the wilderness.

Existentialist? How absurd! For he was merely a young guerrilla fighter, not highly educated, and almost certainly had never heard anyone speak of Existentialism, nor -lacking the ability - ever read any literary works of the Western existentialist school.

In truth, "existence" is not a school of thought. It has been present in human consciousness ever since man first witnessed the death of his fellow beings. It revealed itself in the reflections of soldiers on ancient battlefields, during the endless wars of the Warring States in China, the Middle Ages in the West, and the brutal conquests of Genghis Khan that spread death across the earth.

And that thought - "life is but a temporary lodging, death is the true return" - had already appeared long before Albert Camus wrote *L'Exil et Le Royaume*.

Thus, our "Commune Secretary" also carried in his blood that same awareness of "life is but a temporary lodging, death is the true return," and many times had asked himself about war, about the absurdity of human existence.

Existentialism, in fact, does not originate with Kierkegaard, Dostoevsky, Sartre, or Nietzsche. Its seeds were sown long ago in the works of Laozi, Zhuangzi, and it nearly saturates the Tang poetry of 6th century in China.

So the appearance of this "Existentialist Commune Secretary" is not absurd at all. And from that moment of encounter, I knew he would become the central character in a literary work - the very one you now hold in your hands.

September 15, 2025

DAO HIEU

1.

Father and daughter faced each other in the living room. The father had just returned from a trip, a suitcase in hand. The girl had messy hair, worn-out jeans, a wrinkled shirt, and no jewelry, not even a watch.

"What kind of ridiculous clothes are you wearing?"

"I lost all my clothes."

Mr. Phi Mã laughed loudly, tossing his suitcase onto the armchair.

Phượng opened the fridge, handed her father a can of beer, and took an apple for herself.

"You really lost everything?"

"I gave it all to my friends. Sometimes I get sick of dressing up fancy, all that silly fashion nonsense."

"You don't have a single outfit left besides what you're wearing?"

"No."

Phượng tossed the apple into the trash bin, gazed at her father tenderly:

"Forget it, don't worry. How's work?" "Same as usual. There's a very beautiful Mustang sports car. I think you'd like it."

"I'm fine with the old car."

Mr. Phi Mã removed his jacket and hung it on the chair, loosened his tie. Phượng came up to him, knelt down, and took off his shoes.

"Dad!" Phượng said, "I want to ask you to let me travel for a while."

"You're supposed to be preparing for university exams."

"I'm not taking them anymore."

"But where do you want to go?"

"Duyên Hải."

"What's in Duyên Hải? Just mud everywhere."

"I like it. Just a week."

"You mean right now?"

"I'll just go downtown for a bit now."

Phượng placed his shoes on the rack.

"If you haven't had dinner yet, come eat with me outside."

"I'm not hungry."

"Alright then, I'm off."

Mr. Phi Mã stood at the door, watching his daughter.

The old Toyota 800 shot out from the garage into the yard, startling him. Not because Phượng drove recklessly, but because of the car itself: the front sagging on one side, headlights smashed, windshield cracked.

Phượng leaned out the window, smiling brightly, her sunburned hair glinting. She seemed delighted at her father's shock:

"Are you scared?"

Her father didn't answer. He frowned and asked:

"Who did you crash into?"

"A tree. But no big deal."

"And you're still driving that wreck?"

But the Toyota 800 had already roared out the gate, clattering with the noise of battered metal.

2.

At home, Phượng disliked wearing clothes, so she often wrapped herself in a dark cotton robe while moving around the house. Beneath the robe, everything was unbound, free, swaying with each step.

At ten o'clock, passing the hallway where a tree branch drooped low, she saw that her father had fallen asleep but forgotten to close his door, so she gently pushed it shut. In that motion, she glanced at him and was surprised at how young he looked, despite his thick mustache and graying hair.

The driver, drunk from the afternoon, was snoring loudly.

Phượng wandered to the ylang-ylang tree, searching among its broad dark leaves for a small flower, but found none. The flowers hid somewhere, but their fragrance drifted faintly, luring, caressing.

She stood silently for a long time on the balcony, gazing down at the street. By now traffic had thinned, but the few cars sped past, engines roaring. The noise irritated her, though she herself had often enjoyed speeding that way. Now she thought it childish and ridiculous.

Twenty-two years old. Sorrow had come too soon. It mingled between bursts of explosive joy. Between joy and sorrow was a revolting boredom, that was what Phượng feared most. She wanted to leave, to escape it, erase it.

Her first trip to Duyên Hải had been with the entourage of a senior leader. He was sixty, always eager to prove himself energetic, eloquent, charming. He strode through the mud, gesturing, laughing, and babbling about mangroves and coconut trees. A few agricultural engineers and a geologist accompanied him. They gave their opinions, but the leader argued heatedly: "Wrong! That's just theory, you must rely on folk experience. I say this area can grow coconuts." The agricultural engineer kept silent.

Then Phượng followed the group into Tam Thôn Hiệp commune. The commune secretary was a disabled veteran in his thirties. A man who seemed poorly educated and sluggish. That was her first impression.

When they arrived at the commune office, no one could find him. He should have been there to welcome the delegation, since the visit had been announced in advance. But there was no preparation. Just a thatched hut, bare except for a crude desk, a few wooden chairs, and a bench hidden behind a file cabinet.

The commune secretary was asleep there.

When they woke him, no one realized he was the secretary. His army shirt hung untucked, he was barefoot.

The leader frowned and asked:

"Where's the secretary?"

"Here," he replied without looking at anyone, tossing a filthy pillow into the cabinet.

"Please sit down," he said, dragging the bench to the center.

The leader asked:

"Did you work late last night?"

"No. But whenever I have to wait, I get sleepy. Was there trouble with your boat?"

The leader ignored the question, still standing on the dirt floor, glancing around the shabby room. Others took seats on the bench; many had to stand.

The secretary poured tea into chipped porcelain cups, then rolled tobacco. From the corner, Phượng studied him. Now she noticed he wasn't entirely rustic. Beneath those thick brows were striking eyes—beautiful, bleak, cold. Confidence radiated from his posture, the way he lit his cigarette, especially in his calm, measured voice.

The leader asked again:

"Why don't we see anyone working?"

"Sir, today is Sunday."

The leader laughed louder than the others. He slung an arm around the young secretary's shoulder, squeezing his joints, and asked:

"You're healthy, comrade?"

The secretary didn't answer, as if he hadn't heard. Instead he asked:

"Will you be staying overnight?"

"No," the leader said. "I must return to the district. But surely you can grow coconuts here? We can't leave this land barren!"

The secretary looked out at the glaring yard where a single tall, spindly coconut tree stood.

"That coconut was planted seven years ago. No fruit. I don't know why."

"That's a technical issue," the leader turned to engineer Lâm. "Isn't that right?"

"Yes, sir."

The leader continued:

"I want to turn this area into a coconut island, a center of tourism and industry."

The secretary fixed his eyes on engineer Lâm, and in that moment his gaze brushed against Phượng's. It startled her. Only then did she see the strange brilliance in those eyes.

She thought: Why does he bury his life in this place?

That glance struck her like lightning, followed by thunder that shook the depths of her soul, shattering pride, breaking caution, stirring her from roots to crown.

That extraordinary thunder rumbled on in her spirit for days, months afterward. That rustic man haunted her luxurious life, never fading.

Out on the streets, she often lost track of where she was headed, ran red lights, missed turns. On the stairs, she'd pause: Why am I going up? For what? She once swerved onto a curb, crashing into a tree, the steering wheel thumping her chest.

What's his name? Ridiculous. Why meet again? He wouldn't even remember me. I'd look foolish. Go or not?

*

The driver's snores sounded funny. The city was silent.

"Who's that down on the street?"

Phượng asked, glimpsing a man in a camouflage shirt climbing her gate.

"Who's there?" she called again.

The man lifted his face, bloodied.

"It's Mã Long. Let me in."

Phượng hurried down, speaking through the small hole in the iron gate:

"What happened?"

"They ambushed me. Please, let me in."

"No, my father's home."

"Then take me to the hospital, quick."

Phượng opened the gate, ran to the garage. The battered Toyota 800 shot out. Mã Long closed the gate, slid into the passenger seat.

Phượng drove fast through the night.

Mã Long leaned his bloody face on the window.

"Which hospital?" she asked.

"Forget it, take me to Hùng's house, it's closer."

She swerved at a junction. He lit a cigarette. She glanced, saw him smiling.

"What are you laughing at?"

"Can't I smile?"

"Doesn't it hurt?"

"Of course it does. But I still smile. Where've you been hiding all week?"

"At home. Sleeping."

As she answered, goosebumps prickled her:

she suddenly remembered she was naked beneath her robe. She stopped the car.

"I'm not going to Hùng's."

"Why not?"

"Because I'm not wearing anything underneath. I was about to sleep when you showed up."

Mã Long leaned toward her, then burst out laughing. He didn't look injured at all. He pulled out cotton and a small mirror, wiped away the blood. Within moments his round face was clean, without a single wound.

"What's going on?" Phượng asked.

"An act."

"But why?"

"To get you out. Why've you been avoiding us all week?"

"I'm bored."

"Go out, and boredom will vanish."

"But remember, I have no clothes on." "We'll get you some at Hùng's."

The Toyota 800 sped off again.

At Hùng's house, three men and a fashionable girl were playing cards. Phượng and Mã Long burst in.

"Hello, Titi," Hùng greeted.

"Forget it. Who scripted this stupid act for Mã Long at my place?"

Hùng thumped his chest:

"Me. What's wrong, Titi, are you mad?" "Of course. You scared me."

From the back, Mã Long came out waving a handful of women's underwear in front of Phượng. She grabbed them wordlessly and stormed into the bathroom, under everyone's astonished gaze.

A minute later, she reappeared in baggy jeans.

The group rushed out, piled into her battered car.

At 11 p.m., the Hoa Hồng restaurant was still crowded. The newcomers ordered lavishly. The men drank Hennessy; Phượng and Hùng's girlfriend drank wine. The men ate crudely, gulping liquor, shouting so loudly that nearby diners scowled. Hùng's girlfriend nibbled potatoes delicately like a princess. Phượng devoured steak, drank heavily, laughed loudly. Some foreigners at the next table left.

Phượng grabbed the sleeve of a tall white man:

"You don't look that old."

He shrugged, nearly spilling her wine, then apologized. She pulled him down beside her.

"I'm Italian," he said, "working for UNICEF."

Hùng, with poor English, tried:

"Do you like Mussolini?"

"No," the Italian answered cautiously. "He was a dictator."

"But you like football, right?"

"Of course. Especially the upcoming Mundial in my country."

"You think Italy will win?"

"I think the Netherlands."

Phượng asked:

"What about Connie Francis?"

The Italian looked puzzled.

"Which Francis?"

"You don't know?"

"No."

Phượng exploded, smashing her glass on the floor:

"Shameful! That's shameful!"

Everyone burst out laughing. The Italian bolted, nearly running away.

Past midnight, most customers had gone, the music stopped. Hùng and Mã Long staggered drunk.

"Bill!"

Two waiters brought the check: 450,000.

"What the hell?"

Hùng threw the bill down, rummaged his pockets.

"Not a coin left."

"Forgot my wallet," Mã Long said.

The others shook their heads.

"Put it on the tab," Hùng said. "We're broke."

"Sorry sir, no credit here."

"Why not?" Hùng snapped.

A waiter whispered, "Call brother Hai."

Before he could go, Mã Long blocked him. Plates, glasses crashed to the floor. Wine spilled, tablecloths yanked down, food scattered.

Restaurant staff rushed in, surrounding them. The manager asked:

"What do you want?"

Hùng stood hands on hips, coolly:

"What we wanted, we've already done. Now settle the bill. Four hundred fifty thousand, plus broken dishes, cleanup. How much? One million enough?"

"Enough."

"But we don't have Vietnamese money. Can we pay in dollars?"

"Yes."

Hùng pulled out three $100 bills, handed them over.

"Here. Keep the change as a tip. Sorry, brother."

The manager smiled, shook his hand:

"No problem. Just a little too much to drink. Drive carefully."

3.

"What time did she leave the house?"

"I don't know because I was sleeping very soundly at that time."

"Your driver testified that afternoon he got so drunk that even when someone opened the gate and drove the car out, he didn't notice. Was it true that he went drinking that afternoon?

"Yes."

"Did you hear the dog barking?"

"No. That proves I was dead asleep. And usually when I sleep that deeply, it's around midnight."

"Just now you said she asked your permission to go to Duyên Hải. In your opinion, what was she going there for?"

"For leisure."

"And you believed that?"

"I did."

"Did you recognize the voice on the phone?"

"No. But it was a man's voice."

"And what about your daughter's voice? Was it really Phượng's?"

"Yes."

"Did she cry? Or show any signs of worry, like she was under threat?"

"I heard her voice was calm. But that's always been her nature. She fears no one. She only said: 'Dad, I've been kidnapped. They demand twenty taels of gold as ransom. Prepare it, they'll come to collect.' That was all. Then that man's voice told me they would call back at eight in the morning to give me the time and place for the ransom drop. He threatened to kill my daughter if I informed the police, so I request you absolutely keep this matter secret."

"All right. At eight tomorrow morning, just wait for their call. After that, report the details to us at the private number I gave you earlier."

*

Mr. Phi Mã paid for the coffee, stood up, left the café, hailed a cycle rickshaw, and headed toward downtown.

The kidnappers had promised to call at eight, but the director of Phi Mã Car Company didn't receive their call until nearly ten o'clock.

"I've prepared everything," he said. "Tell me the location for the delivery."

"It's not that simple" - the man on the phone replied - First you must follow our instructions. At noon today go to Đức Bà church, the fifth pew by the aisle. There you'll find a letter. Do exactly as it says. Absolutely no police, or your daughter's life won't be guaranteed."

At noon, Mr. Phi Mã followed the kidnappers' instructions and indeed found a slip of paper hidden under the pew.

"Leave the church, look toward the post office, and you'll see a motorbike taxi driver on a Honda, wearing a short-sleeved black shirt. He will take you to us."

Mr. Phi Mã stepped out of the church and immediately spotted the rider. The man bowed and said:

"Please get on."

Without a word, clutching the leather briefcase to his chest, he climbed on. The motorbike sped toward Chợ Lớn.

He was taken on a long detour around Chợ Bình Tây, then disappeared into the bustling trading streets.

The kidnappers' diversion was clever, but it did not escape the eyes of the criminal police. The four-man surveillance team, handguns concealed, approached an old townhouse deep in an alley and suddenly kicked the door open.

Inside was a messy room strewn with cushions, blankets, empty bottles, beer cans, cups, cigarettes. Phượng was fast asleep on a velvet sofa, the young men sprawled around her on mats and on the floor. All were sleeping peacefully as if nothing had happened. Ông Phi Mã sat silently in an armchair facing his beloved daughter.

The police officers stood dumbfounded, useless pistols in hand.

"Why is this?" Mt. Phi Mã asked.

"Wake her up," one officer said.

He sat beside her.

"Phượng! Wake up, my dear. Phượng!"

She stirred, opened her eyes, and smiled when she saw her father.

"What kind of game is this?" he asked.

"Sorry, Dad. We just wanted to play a little prank."

"How could you? You've troubled so many people. Apologize to the officers."

"This is no matter of apology," an officer said.

"All of you are under arrest for mocking the law. Search the house!"

The sleepers were kicked awake. Before they could react, they were handcuffed and shoved into a corner.

"Who is the homeowner?" asked the police.

"I am," Hùng replied.

"Come with us."

Cupboards were opened, mattresses overturned, pillows ripped. They found a small vial of heroin hidden among the clothes.

"Sign the record," the officer ordered.

Hùng scrawled his name without hesitation.

"Who invented the kidnapping story?"

"That was Phượng's idea."

"Why did you do it?"

"We were bored. Wanted some fun."

A harsh slap landed on Hùng's face. Phượng jumped up:

"What are you doing? Who gave you the right to hit him?"

"No arguments," the officer snapped. "All of you, to the station."

Mr. Phi Mã pleaded that his daughter not be handcuffed, but still felt humiliated walking past the curious crowd gathered outside.

4.

What annoyed Phượng most in the interrogation room was the handsome face of Captain Tùng. He seemed overly confident about his looks. Each time he thought he said something witty, he would squint like an actor, convinced that this little gesture could melt any girl's heart. His styled hair and overly polished clothes also infuriated her. She wanted to tell him not to delude himself—that he was nothing more than a castrated rooster—yet she had to sit there listening to his questions and answer them word by word.

"Give me your arm."

Phượng placed her hand on the table before him.

"Pull up your sleeve!"

"What for?" she frowned.

"Here only I have the right to ask questions. You do not. Pull it up!"

She rolled her sleeve above the elbow. He leaned in, studied her arm, then asked:

"Do you know about AIDS?"

"That disease doesn't exist in Việt Nam yet."

"Not so sure. Let me tell you, junkies spread AIDS. I see injection marks on your arm."

"Those are mosquito bites."

"Mosquito bites..." he muttered. "Then why did you fabricate a kidnapping?"

Why did he think that was so important? It was nothing. She was bored, wanted to stir things up. That's all. But many people refused to believe such a simple reason. They suspected conspiracies, dark mysteries. Truly, some things in this world cannot be explained with words. They require a hammer, a blow. Otherwise people just keep asking: 'Why are you bored? You're young, beautiful, rich. A villa, a car, servants at your call, why bored?"

That question, repeated endlessly, drove Phượng mad:

"Shut up, Captain. If I were a peasant girl with muddy feet, illiterate, munching snacks all day, perhaps I wouldn't be bored. If I had a handsome husband like you, perhaps I wouldn't be bored. If I were a police captain sitting high and mighty interrogating others, perhaps I wouldn't be bored. If I suddenly turned into a castrated rooster, maybe that would be even more fun!"

Tùng slammed the table.

"What are you saying? Do you realize where you are? I ask, you must answer seriously."

"Go ahead then."

"Whether I ask or not is my choice. You're still young. Your father is a respected businessman in this city. You must protect his honor, you must care for him. Do you know how he suffered when he heard you'd been kidnapped? He came to me in tears, cigarette trembling in his hand, his face ashen. Three days later I met him again, he looked like an old man of eighty. And I myself lost sleep for nights because of you, because of your prank. Why would you act so irresponsibly?"

Phượng sighed.

"I don't want your moral lessons. I just want to know what charge you're pressing and how many years in prison. That's all."

"The punishment is secondary. The point is for you to realize your wrongdoing. Do you not see it? Using your own honorable father in such a prank—isn't that wrong?"

"But what if I enjoy doing such things because I no longer believe in anything, then what?"

He smirked, exhaled smoke toward the ceiling.

"If you think that way, you could become a danger to society. People won't let you do whatever you want."

Phượng turned her palms upward, showing him.

"Since ancient times kings and mandarins did ridiculous things just because they held power. I don't, so here I sit, being interrogated by you."

Tùng stubbed his cigarette and looked at her with mockery and pity.

"Don't be stubborn, little sister. I understand you better than you do yourself. That's why I want to let you off. In fact, I'd like us to be friends. I have no wish to press charges."

"Thanks," Phượng said. "What do I do now?"

He handed her papers.

"Sign the statement. Tomorrow you'll be released."

She signed quickly, then left the room, irritated by his smugness. He wanted to prove her wrong, while she wanted the opposite: to make him submit, to expose all his flaws before her, so that she could sit in his chair and ask: "Wrong or Right?" That was the ridiculous game she longed to play with him.

But not yet. For now, that game was playing out with Hùng and Mã Long in that other room.

*

Whether a case was deemed serious often depended not so much on evidence but on outside factors. Deceiving the police, possessing opium, five years, ten years, or acquittal? It was like a three-card trick. All Phượng knew was that the next day she was released. Mr. Phi Mã came in his Mercedes to pick her up. A week later, Mã Long, Hùng, and the rest were freed as well. They were cheerful, but Phượng was disheartened. She had always thought she had the right to her reckless stunts and that others would admire her defiance. But now she knew some saw them as crimes, others with pity. That, she could not accept. Sitting in her father's Mercedes, she thought of how to defeat that man.

But once home, all plans evaporated when she faced her father in his private room. He said nothing, but wept. It was the second time she had ever seen him cry. The first was when her mother died. After the mourners left, just the two of them sat by the coffin in the brightly lit, incense-filled room, and he wept with his face in his hands. Now again, just the two of them. Both times Phượng had been calm, no tears, no sadness, only a flood of remorse.

Why remorse at her mother's death? She had not caused it, bore no responsibility. Yet she had felt anguish as if guilty. Perhaps because she couldn't bear witnessing a life's departure, that powerless feeling before death. Her prideful, defiant self had wanted to rebel, but against whom?

She had told herself: This cannot be accepted. Death made her angry, more than sorrowful, so the tears never came. Her eyes burned dry, her mouth bitter. That was her first encounter with death: cruel, absurd, grotesque. Her mother's once-beautiful face turned into lifeless clay, her tender eyes frozen like those of a stupid old doll. That was not her mother's fault. Whose fault was it? No answer. Anger erupted in sobs, born of grief, compassion, and rage. She was eight. Lonely, bewildered, lost.

Now, in this luxurious room, no one had died, but her father wept again, quiet, miserable as before.

"I'm sorry, Dad."

He wiped his tears, trembling and feeble.

"Phượng, I never imagined this would happen. I've spoiled you too much because I always believed in you."

"Do you regret that?"

"But why did you befriend such people? Do you know who they are? Smugglers, hoodlums. Do you know why they too were released? Because I wanted this ended quickly, erased from your memory. And you must erase them too. Tell me, what do you want? What do you need? I'll give it."

"I want to escape the monotony. Can you bear it, Dad? That absurdity rules over people, wields power. That's vile, ridiculous, unforgivable."

"What absurdity?"

She leapt up, in tears.

"Open the window, look at the street, you'll see absurdity parading by. It's everywhere, in praise, in condemnation. It's unbearable! Give me a bomb and I'll throw it in its face. Let me go!"

She sobbed, shaking.

Mr. Phi Mã placed a hand on her shoulder.

"Ignore it. Do you think I don't see? I just don't care. Live your own life. You will have everything, my dear."

Phượng knelt, hugging his legs.

"Thank you, Ba. Thank you."

He stroked her sun-bleached hair.

"Go rest. I must go to the office."

When he left, she didn't go upstairs but lay in the living room. Noon was quiet, empty. She felt defeated, returning alone. Suddenly the face of the commune secretary she had once met in Duyên Hải came to her. His gaze carried immense solitude, hiding a lifetime's tragedies. She felt he wanted the officials to leave his swampy land quickly. His indifference had irritated the city leader, who led the group back to the boat. The secretary didn't see them off; he just stood in his hut, smoking, watching them leave. A cool breeze rose from the river. Phượng passed by.

"You don't seem from here?" she asked.

"I came from far away."

"You seem... different."

He smiled, innocently surprised:

"Really?"

"I imagine you should be someone else, in another place."

"Don't mind. Wherever we are, it's all temporary. Go on, they're boarding."

But the leader was still chatting by the riverside, so she lingered.

"What do you think of that leader?"

"He looks too enthusiastic. It worries me."

"Poor man," she said, waving goodbye to the secretary, then walked to the river.

It was the strangest noon of her life. The sun pale and cold, the breeze faint, brushing her hair, the riverside leaves.

She boarded the boat, looked back, and saw him still alone beneath the thatched roof. The dry straws trembled in the wind, but his thin figure remained still.

That image etched itself in her memory.

Now, in her room, she pressed play on the cassette. Gentle music filled the air, recalling that chilly river breeze.

5.

Captain Tùng sat still, face cold. He didn't look at anyone, didn't talk to anyone, as if he were sitting among weeds, trash, and dry wood. He smoked absentmindedly. Vân poured beer and offered it to him, but Tùng didn't move, didn't respond.

"Cheer up a little, or else my friends will feel awkward," she said.

Still, Tùng didn't budge, didn't speak. Vân had to start small talk to break the silence.

"Thúy looks beautiful in that dress today."

"Don't flatter me," the friend replied, "my husband always complains."

"When did I ever complain?" her husband said. "In my eyes, my wife is the most beautiful woman in the world." Then he turned to Tùng:

"You don't look well, do you?"

Tùng only curled his lip slightly, nothing more, not even glancing at the man trying to strike up conversation. Vân tried to salvage the situation with a bright smile:

"He's upset because I don't have a dress as pretty as Thúy's."

Everyone laughed at that remark, but Tùng still sat like a refrigerator. Vân whispered in his ear:

"I beg you. Everyone here are my business friends. Don't make me lose face with them."

Only then did Tùng turn to his wife:

"Let's go home!"

"We can't. The bride and groom are my best friend's siblings. We already arrived late, if we leave early it'll look bad. Raise a glass with my friends."

"I said let's go home!"

"At least wait until we give our gift to the bride and groom."

Tùng stood up immediately, strode to the gift table, pulled out a thick envelope and placed it there, then stood waiting right at the spot for his wife.

Vân had no choice but to rise:

"I'm sorry, everyone. I don't know what's wrong with my husband today. Please don't be offended."

The men stayed cold, while the women looked irritated. One said:

"Who does he think he is, acting so arrogant?"

Just then the bride and groom came over. "Chị Vân! Where are you going?"

"I'm just stepping out to see a relative, I'll be right back."

And Vân disappeared.

*

Back home, Vân exploded:

"What the hell was that? You're not a minister, not anyone's father. Don't look down on people so much. Do you think anyone will want to do business with me now?"

"Shut up! I told you, I don't like drinking with that flea-market crowd. Just seeing them makes me want to vomit."

"And who do you think you are, to be so arrogant? You think being a captain makes you great?"

"Great or not, doesn't matter. But I despise those people."

"You despise them, do you think they respect you? Do you know what my friends say about you? That you're a man hiding behind your wife's skirt, acting high and mighty. You think you're talented? What talent? Try leaving this family, let's see if you still get perfume, canned beer, Western liquor to use. You look down on the flea market, huh? But the money you're spending is flea-market money."

Tùng was holding a brand-new aluminum kettle full of boiling water. Angered by her words, he wanted to hurl it, but afraid the water would splash back, he climbed onto a stool instead and dropped it on the floor. Water splashed everywhere, the lid popped off, circled the stool, and flipped upside down.

"You say another word and I'll smash the TV."

"Ha! As if. A man like you wouldn't dare. If you smash the TV, I'll walk out on my head."

Tùng stood, pointed at his wife's face, and shouted:

"Get out! Don't talk flea-market nonsense to me."

"I may be flea-market, but my manners aren't flea-market. You're a Party member, an official, yet you count every penny. When my parents came from the countryside to visit, you didn't even want to host them. They stayed only three days, and you asked: 'Why are they staying so long?' Coward!"

Tùng kicked the aluminum kettle toward Vân. She dodged to the side, laughed loudly, then stormed out and slammed the door.

*

Late afternoon, Tùng woke from a long nap. His wife still hadn't come home, which worried him a little. He told his child:

"Stay here and wait for your mother. Daddy has something to do."

He drove his La Dalat straight to the Labor Cultural House, where he had an appointment to play tennis with a friend. The parking lot was crowded, so he maneuvered for a while before finding a spot. Just as he stopped, before opening the door — *bam!* — his face slammed against the steering wheel. Furious, Tùng jumped out. His freshly refurbished La Dalat had been rear-ended by an old sedan, crushing the trunk and shattering all the rear lights and signals. The other car's front was also smashed. Enraged, Tùng rushed to yank open its door. A woman's voice called:

"Wait, wait, don't get angry."

A young woman stepped out, hands on her hips, looking at the two cars locked together, giggling.

"Ah, Tùng!" Phượng waved cheerfully. "What luck to meet you again."

"And for me, what bad luck to meet you again. What kind of driving is this?"

"The brakes failed. But don't worry. I know a dozen garages in Sài Gòn. Sorry about this. Let's go fix it."

"You're wasting my time."

Phượng led Tùng to a garage on Nguyễn Trãi street. Tùng grimaced at his crumpled car.

"My car was just repaired less than two weeks ago."

Phượng handed him a stick of chewing gum.

"Regretting it? Your car's outdated anyway. Time to throw it in the trash."

"You're the daughter of a car company owner, yet you drive a wreck. What about me?"

"That's because I'm reckless. You're not reckless—you're an official."

"But I'm not rich like you. This car is precious to me."

"Don't worry. I'll have them fix it better than before. This time just patch it up, next time I'll hit harder so we can 'scrap' both cars and get new ones."

"'We'?!" Tùng gawked at the girl blowing bubbles like a child.

"Yes, *we.*" Phượng emphasized. "That means you and me."

"Oh no, spare me. This will take a week."

Phượng tossed a pack of Dunhill to the mechanic.

"Sunday pickup, okay? Both cars."

"Ten days at least. Even if we work day and night."

Phượng pulled out a wad of five-thousand bills and handed it to the garage owner. She offered Tùng a cigarette.

"Are you free now?"

"I was supposed to be playing tennis."

"Let me take you to dinner. My way of apologizing. Please?"

Tùng glanced at the street.

"With what car?"

Before Phượng could answer, the garage owner offered:

"Take my Cub. Return it anytime."

They had dinner at the Độc Lập Hotel, then went dancing.

Tùng was surprised at how easily he was swept along by this young woman. Phượng had something wild yet poetic, brazen yet tender. Her recklessness and femininity blended naturally, making it impossible for Tùng to resist.

They held each other in a shadowy corner under dim purple light.

Tùng asked:

"Why were you so stubborn when I interrogated you?"

"Because I hated your sanctimonious attitude. If only you had been like now, it would have been better."

"Not necessarily. Back then I had to act that way."

"You could've been different. For example, don't preach morality. That's the police's biggest mistake. But now, you're great. You dance very well."

"You're great too. I never thought you'd be this gentle, especially the way you tilt your head. I think you'd look stunning in a dress."

"Maybe. But I prefer wearing something rough, a bit dusty. It makes me feel free."

"Did you go to a French school?"

"I was born in France. Came back to Việt Nam at fifteen, when my mother died. Since then, it's just me and my father, living like friends."

Tùng said:

"My family wasn't French, but we were from the Nguyễn dynasty's royal lineage. So back in the jungle I used to joke I was an aristocratic communist. I wasn't really proletarian. We had villas, cars, gold by the kilo, not tael. Yet I still joined the resistance. The others hated me for it, said I was petty bourgeois."

"Because you looked down on them, right?"

"No. Because they were childish. You wouldn't believe how ridiculous it was. One time I picked a red flower by the stream and put it in a glass of water. The security guard kept glaring. That evening, when I came back from a meeting, the flower was on the ground, trampled."

"Childish!"

"Countless stories like that. I had a friend from Sài Gòn, poor but studious. Oddly, his parents named him Đặng Hoa Kỳ (USA). He was diligent, politically sound, good at his work. When they proposed him for Party membership, his application was rejected. Reason: the Party couldn't admit someone named after U.S. imperialism. The poor guy cried. He compared himself to me: why could I, a descendant of Emperor Đồng Khánh, join, while he was rejected just for his name? The whole unit laughed. Still, his membership was delayed until after liberation. In 1978, someone advised him to drop the 'Kỳ' and go by Đặng Hoa. Then his file was processed again. But just then, China invaded the northern border. His application was rejected again. Reason: the Party couldn't admit someone named after the expansionist Chinese (Hoa), especially with the surname Đặng (Deng Xiaoping)."

While dancing, Phượng doubled over laughing, clapped her hand over her mouth, and ran back to the table. Luckily the music shifted to loud Soul, so no one noticed.

Strobe lights flashed like ghosts. Phượng saw Tùng's face flickering among the writhing, puppet-like crowd.

She drained her beer, crushed the can in her hand. She felt lucky to be alive, an entirely new sensation. Perhaps it was the absurdity of others, their envy, that gave her joy. Maybe that was it. Each time she witnessed absurdity, she felt exhilarated, full of happiness.

Phượng cracked open another beer, downed it in one gulp. She looked at Tùng dancing in the crowd and laughed dryly. He would be the most expensive toy of her life, the absurdity she would peel layer by layer until he was bare. Then she would sit on the other side of the interrogation table and ask: *True or false?*

6.

Phượng brought coffee for the guests - her father's guests - all important figures of the city.

The sun had already risen, but its rays had not yet reached the lawn in the yard because the sun was still caught in the tall trees behind the house.

The director of the automobile company received his guests outside in the yard. They sat around a round marble table placed under the trees: a professor with a doctorate, a monk, a writer, a director of publishing, and Captain Tùng.

But to Phượng, they were nothing more than spoiled children.

That was how she saw them when they ate the food she brought. Their eyes lit up, their mouths smiling brightly. Even the way they chewed bread looked amusing, their mustaches twitching playfully. The way they gulped coffee was charming, and above all, the way they smoked, at once arrogant and ridiculous. Who could have invented such a habit, taking dried leaves, rolling them up, burning them, and inhaling the smoke? The habit was at once civilized and barbaric. That was why, when watching someone smoke, sometimes they looked elegant, and other times they looked absurd.

As for their conversations, Phượng usually withdrew. Their topics never had anything to do with her life. But this time, she couldn't escape. Her father had pulled her to sit beside him. In fact, their conversation had started before the water for coffee had even boiled. By the time Phượng arrived, it was still lively.

Someone said:

"The Romanian Ceausescu is more ridiculous than the feudal emperors of China. Every day he wears a new suit, and once he wears it, the suit is wrapped, sealed, and thrown into the incinerator. What is he trying to prove?"

"It's just showing off," Phượng said. "Some leaders in Vietnam like to wear patched shirts. Gandhi was shirtless."

Her father, Phi Mã, patted her back.

"When leaders show off, people praise them as saints. But when my daughter shows off, she gets scolded all the time."

Phượng protested:

"I don't show off."

"Then why do you insist on driving that old, dented, broken-down car?"

"Driving a car is just like wearing clothes. If it's too fancy, you lose your freedom."

The publishing director joined in:

"In Europe, anyone driving a junk car like that gets fined. And the car companies sue them. Look at my car: the latest Toyota model."

"That's because you're a director. You need a luxury car."

"Not anymore. I'm no longer a director."

This was breaking news that none of the guests had heard yet.

Tùng asked:

"You requested a transfer?"

"No," the man said. "I resigned. With Eastern Europe collapsing, all values overturned, why cling to official titles?"

The monk asked:

"So what will you do now?"

"Just be an ordinary citizen. But I'll still publish books. If I print ten thousand copies of a good book, I'll make money without responsibility."

The writer said:

"I think our country will also change. You're an old student activist, you ought to do something."

The publishing director grinned, showing his teeth stained black with tobacco smoke.

"Oh, I will. My plan has three steps. Step one, resign as director. Step two, leave the Party. Step three, wait for the right time to stir things up."

"You'll be a character in one of my novels," the writer said. "This era belongs to novels—so much chaos, so much drama."

The director replied:

"Then I'll commission you right now to write me a novel like this: You go to a factory, do some research, and come up with a plot that proves production would actually develop better without Party leadership. Can you do that? I'll advance you two million."

"But who would grant permission? Who would dare?"

"I'll handle that. Remember, I have influence with the publishers. I'll fund it myself. Ten thousand copies guaranteed, all sold. Can you do it?"

"Of course. But how long?"

"Two hundred fifty to three hundred pages. Naturally, it should include some romance. A love story blossoming through struggle."

The writer waved him off.

"Don't meddle in my craft."

The director slapped his forehead.

"And here's another moneymaker. I've just found a copy of *Việt Nam Sử Lược* by Trần Trọng Kim. Could you handle this?"

"Go on," the writer urged.

"I'll let you read it. You take the historical events and create characters and romances — like *Tiêu Sơn Tráng Sĩ* — maybe even a love story between a Vietnamese hero and a Chinese beauty. In short, invent and imagine boldly. Write me a whole series of Vietnamese martial arts novels. I bet 1990 will be the year of the martial arts novel. Getting licenses for Chinese martial arts novels is difficult, but for Vietnamese ones, it's easy. Writing that kind of thing also sells. Can you do it?"

The writer looked thoughtful.

"I've never written that genre. I still prefer tackling the hot issues of today's life. But honestly, writing martial arts novels wouldn't be hard."

Phượng lit a cigarette for the writer and asked:

"Would you ever write the 'purple flower' kind of novels?"

"Oh!" the writer exclaimed. "That used to be my specialty, the sweet love stories of adolescence. Beautiful poems, really, little girl."

"So why don't you keep writing them now?"

"Because the era we live in places enormous issues before writers: the crisis of faith, the collapse of character, the overturning of moral values, the crumbling of political foundations... The writer is a witness of his time."

Phượng interrupted him:

"I'm a witness too. There's nothing more interesting than being a witness. A witness is just like a spectator, and life is a vast stage."

The writer faltered, as though thrown off balance. He fell silent, wondering if there was some hidden meaning in the rebellious girl's words. Phượng stood up to make tea.

The professor turned to her father:

"Your daughter is very intelligent."

Phi Mã laughed:

"Yet she's the worst student. Failed the university entrance exam three times."

"Well then, you must know what she wants," the professor said.

"Even she doesn't know what she wants, let alone me. Seems like all young people these days are like that."

"Not necessarily," the professor replied.

"Many of my students are good, diligent, ambitious. I care for them, but when a student is too good, too obedient, I find them dim, almost pitiful. The irony is that in backward countries, such dim types often dominate society. In China, for example, it was children who terrorized a billion people during the Cultural Revolution. The power of stupidity is more terrifying than bombs. Don't you all agree?"

"Absolutely," Tùng said passionately. "I too was a resistance fighter, a communist Party member, but I suffered bitterly from such stupidity. That's why we must eliminate fools from the Party. We must build a completely new Communist Party. That is an irresistible trend."

The professor squinted mockingly:

"I can't imagine what a new Communist Party would look like. What economic direction would it take? What kind of political activity? What about culture, arts, journalism, education? What model in the world are you talking about?"

While Tùng was still flustered by the professor's questions, Phượng brought tea, smiling as she poured.

"That's my model," she said lightly. "If any writer were to write about my life, that would be the new communist model: no private property, no state. Simply put, the way of the vagabond."

The professor burst out laughing.

"That's an idea. At least you're smarter than most of my students."

Phượng carried the tray of coffee cups away. At the far end of the lawn she dropped a few small spoons and fumbled awkwardly to pick them up. Tùng rushed to help. As they both bent down, Phượng whispered:

"Come out with me Sunday morning."

"Where?"

"Thủ Đức. In your car. Same meeting place."

Tùng returned to the table. The professor was continuing on another subject:

"From the Middle Ages until the 18th century in Europe, Christianity was a powerful political party. Over time it weakened, but it was never destroyed. It transformed into ritual, into cultural movement, and throughout nearly two thousand years of history it gave humanity magnificent cultural and artistic achievements: Gothic and Baroque architecture, great sculptures, priceless frescoes, and a classical music tradition never equaled, irreplaceable. It produced geniuses like Michelangelo, Raphael, Beethoven, Mozart..."

From behind the villa came a strange sound mixed with Phượng's laughter. Everyone fell silent, listening.

"What is that?" Tùng asked.

Phi Mã smiled.

"Guess."

While the others were puzzled, a small bear burst from behind a clump of oleanders, with Phượng chasing after it, whip in hand. Dressed like a circus performer, she laughed as she chased the bear. The bear darted to the magnolia tree and scrambled up swiftly. Standing below, Phượng hid the whip behind her back and held out a lump of sugar.

"Come down, Misa!"

The bear climbed down and rolled on the grass. Phượng popped the sugar into its mouth.

"Where did the bear come from?" the monk asked.

"I bought it in Đà Lạt," said Phi Mã. "It's been tamed. My girl doesn't like cats or dogs. She wanted a lion, but when she met this bear, she was delighted. Cost me two million."

"One day if she wants to start a circus troupe, don't be surprised," the writer said.

"I won't," Phi Mã laughed. "I've even thought that one day she might burn this house down."

He spoke cheerfully, without a trace of concern.

On the lawn, the little bear rolled on command under Phượng's whip.

THE CLOWN – Dao Hieu

*

That evening, on the city circus stage, there was also a small bear. It wore a tight, bright red jacket. But the one handling it was a clown with a round nose like a tomato and a wide pink mouth stretching to his ears. He wore a gaudy sleeveless shirt and baggy striped pants.

The clown handled the bear clumsily. When he ordered it to stand, it lay down. When he told it to roll left, it rolled right. At last, he gave up, slumping on a ball. Then the bear grabbed the whip and smacked him on the backside. Startled, he leapt onto the ball, rolled it frantically across the stage. In his panic, the red tomato nose fell to the ground.

The bear picked it up, stopped chasing, and sat like a child, nibbling at the tomato. The clown hopped down, eyeing it hungrily but afraid to snatch it back. Finally he held out his hand, and the bear shared a seed with him.

Just then a beautiful girl rushed out from backstage, whip in hand. The bear quickly stood on its hind legs and bowed. She tossed it a small bicycle, then flipped onto the back seat as the bear pedaled away.

The audience applauded wildly while the clown stood bewildered in the spotlight.

Phượng turned to her father.

"What do you think of that clown?"

"Not bad. He makes people laugh without being vulgar."

"Look at his bewildered expression. Like a stranger from another planet."

Onstage, the clown now performed with a magician who was producing chicks by the dozen from his bowler hat. Phượng didn't care for the trick. She preferred to observe the performers.

"Father," she whispered, "if only that clown were really short, he'd be even better."

But her father was already drowsy, eyelids drooping behind his glasses.

"Tired, Father?" she asked.

"Let's go. Nothing worth watching in these clown shows."

"I only came to see the animal acts anyway," she said.

7.

Tùng arrived at the café five minutes early, but Phượng was already there waiting. They headed straight for Thu Duc.

Phượng asked:

"Did they fix the car to your liking?" "It's fine."

Tùng accelerated.

"What happened at home?"

"Nothing."

"I can tell you're sad."

"Sad for five minutes."

"And after five minutes?"

"It will be the rubber forest. Do you like rubber forests?"

"No. I like to see something barren and desolate."

Tùng slowed the car.

"Then why bother going far?"

"I want to find ownerless graves, to see how desolate they are."

Tùng laughed.

"Alright. I'll take you to visit Dam Tien's grave. But why such a strange idea? At home I imagined a completely different kind of date."

Phượng rummaged through her travel bag, pulled out a can of beer, and handed it to Tùng. Evening fell. The sunlight grew pale, drifting across clouds and treetops, while the ground cooled.

Tùng stopped the car when he saw a small trail leading into a barren hilly area, the land uneven like a graveyard, covered with thorny grass, cactus, and wild grapes. A black crow had just landed on a bare grave. The evening wind blew forlornly across the tall grasses, through Phượng's sunburnt hair. She walked ahead, bewildered like a lost animal. The mounds were silent, swept by wind; even the birds' cries were faint, strange, and lonely. The sky stretched vast, streaked with pink clouds as thin as a floating veil. The earth seemed mute, yet alive again after lying parched all day under burning sun. On the winding path, lizards and musk rats began hunting for food. They froze to stare at the intruders, making odd noises. Black crows circled overhead.

Tùng paid no attention to the crows. He climbed a mound, scanning for a patch of green or some flat spot where he could sit with her, push her down, and make love. He checked if there were signs of people around. Ahead lay a sparse cassava field, with a tiny hut. It seemed abandoned—no lamps lit. He thought he could bring Phượng there. A tryst inside that hut might be thrilling.

"Have you ever been inside a hut like that?"

Tùng asked.

"Never. It's like a stilt house, isn't it?"

"Almost. We'll go in later."

Phượng looked at the sky, absentmindedly:

"I'd like to sleep overnight there."

A chill ran down Tùng's spine—not fear, but surprise that made him want to shiver. He held her hand.

"Aren't you afraid?"

"No."

But Tùng was afraid.

"You really mean to stay overnight there?"

"Yes."

"But my car? I can't just leave it here in the middle of nowhere."

"You're afraid it'll get stolen? Even better if it does."

Tùng tossed a pebble onto her hair.

"Do you like this scenery?"

"No. I only like it because you're here.

Phượng, let's go to that hut."

Phượng smiled:

"Impatient, are you?"

"No. But sitting here forever is boring."

They both stood. Phượng said:

"Before we visit the hut, I want to give you a surprise. Stand still. Don't turn around. When I say 'done,' then you may look."

Tùng's heart pounded, he had never felt such thrilling suspense. What surprise would this spirited girl give him?

"I'll obey," Tùng said. "I'll even close my eyes."

"Yes. Turn your back, close your eyes. Begin now."

Behind him, he heard the sound of a zipper, then rustling, footsteps shifting.

"Not yet," Phượng said, giggling.

More footsteps, more rustling, like clothes being removed. Time teased Tùng, mocking him. Finally came the words he awaited:

"Done."

Tùng spread his arms, turned around, and faced roaring flames. His La Dalat car was ablaze. Fire leapt skyward. Phượng burst out laughing, grabbed his hand.

"Run! It's about to explode!"

Tùng was shocked, terrified, unable to believe his eyes. He had no time to react, only to stumble after Phượng like a man possessed. Only when they stopped did he realize they had entered the hut beside the cassava field.

"What the hell are you doing?" he shouted.

Phượng stood watching the distant fire, then calmly said:

"A car like yours, in Japan, people dump in the junkyard."

Tùng snapped:

"Dump or not, that's my business. I just rebuilt the engine and spent three million dong refurbishing it. This is no joke!"

"Trash," Phượng said. "You'll get a new one. You've lost nothing."

"Don't mock me."

"Never. Perhaps this is the moment I should speak frankly, if you allow."

"Go on."

"I'm a very rich and practical woman. I like you. So, do you want to be my husband? I'm my father's only child. We will live in luxury. But I will not be anyone's mistress. You have one week to decide."

Tùng sat silently in the dark, lit a cigarette.

Mosquitoes whined though the wind blew strong.

At last Phượng sat beside him on the bamboo bed against the wall. Suddenly Tùng grabbed her, kissing her neck fiercely, forcing her down violently.

But his arm was twisted painfully behind his back; agony shot through him as he rolled, still trapped in her hold.

"Let go! It hurts!"

But Phượng did not release him.

"Don't decide until you've thought carefully," she said.

8.

That night Phượng dressed extravagantly, like a nightclub dancer. She bought a front-row ticket at the circus, chewing gum while watching the clown. He was dull tonight, only the children laughed. His disappointment gave him an oddly quiet air that clashed with his painted clown face, making him ridiculous.

At one point, the audience grew so silent that he panicked. He pulled a red scarf from his pocket, waved it, grinning. He showed it was an ordinary scarf, tied a knot, pulled hard on both ends. Then he went down to the audience.

Phượng's flashy outfit caught his eye. He stopped in front of her, handed her the scarf, asking her to tie another knot and test it. Feeling sorry for him, she obliged. He thanked her and moved to a young man, who also tied a knot. Then the clown returned to the stage. He pulled on the scarf, shook his head in mock helplessness, then suddenly with a gentle tug all the knots slipped free. Applause.

The volunteer turned to leave, but the clown called him back. From his pocket, the clown produced a wristwatch. The audience roared with laughter at his quick fingers. But the man waved it off:

"Not mine."

Phượng suddenly realized her own wrist was bare, her Casio was gone. She stood. The clown bent, returned the watch to her. Thunderous applause. Phượng shook his hand.

"You're a genius."

"Thank you. But I'm just a clown."

He slipped backstage.

The next act was trapeze, which Phượng didn't enjoy. She left. Outside, she spotted the clown sitting at a stone table behind the tent, drinking water. She approached.

"Will you perform again tonight?"

"My part is done."

Phượng offered him a cigarette.

"When did you take my watch?"

"When I handed you the scarf."

"I didn't notice at all."

"Because you were focused on the scarf."

"No," Phượng said. "Because you're a very skilled thief."

The clown lit his cigarette, smiling. But with his red-painted mouth stretched to his ears, the smile looked grotesque.

"Do you think I could pickpocket in the marketplace?"

"Easily. If you dare, I'll be your apprentice."

"But if we fail?"

"I'll support you in prison. But you're leaving soon, aren't you?"

"Yes."

"Why not remove the tomato nose and wash your face?"

"Because I'm ugly. I don't want the audience to know my face."

"Not true."

"It is. I'm the only performer whose audience doesn't know my face. Others are recognized on the street. I'm free because I'm not. That's my freedom."

Phượng laughed.

"Maybe I've met you somewhere already."

"Very possible," he said.

"How can I recognize you if we meet outside?"

"Why would you want to?"

"I want to see your real face."

"You'd be disappointed. Besides, I prefer to hide it, to create a legend. That's one of life's tricks. I'm a clown, I must know such tricks."

Phượng:

"But if you understood me, you wouldn't need a legend. I'll drive you crazy."

"And I'll make you laugh. Then you can't drive me crazy."

Phượng checked her watch, rose.

"Goodbye. If I stay, I'll make you crazy—and that means you lose."

"Thank you. Next time I'll try harder to make you laugh."

She left for the parking lot, gave the gate guard a pack of cigarettes, drove inside. Several motorbikes stood parked, but no guests around. She walked past the corridor, by the video room, door shut. She paused, then kept going. Upstairs, through the vent, she glimpsed the familiar guests watching sex films on the small screen. She changed clothes, bathed, but the heat lingered. She went down to the garden, reclined behind an oleander bush. The night was calm, stars sparse but bright.

Around eleven, the video room opened, guests departed. She saw her father cheerful as a boy, the monk solemn, the professor absentminded, the publishing director chatting excitedly with the district chairman. No one noticed her hidden in the leaves. Phi Mã saw them out, still smiling, then returned. Phượng called softly:

"Father."

"Oh, when did you get back?"

"Long ago."

"Why lie there? Something troubling you?"

Phượng gazed skyward, dreamy.

"What film were they watching so secretly?"

"A documentary on the Romanian and Eastern European revolutions. We had to shut the door for the air conditioner."

"And the monk's opinion?"

"He's progressive, liberal—a rare man. Of course he supports the revolution."

"And the writer?"

"I think he could be a minister... well, never mind."

"Don't bother. What about the district chairman? He's a Communist darling, long-time Party member. What's his stance?"

"He's a progressive Communist. Loyal to the Party, convinced socialism will triumph, but he accepts the others. They're close friends."

Phượng walked with her father back inside. He patted her back.

"And you? Which side do you like?" Phượng looked at him, eyes playful, mocking: "I only like the clown. Do you remember the circus clown? I just met him. While talking, he stole my watch without me knowing."

Phi Mã laughed loudly. They parted at the stairs.

"Goodnight, father."

"Don't be sad. I'll buy you another watch."

*

The next day at Vũng Tàu beach, Phượng again met her father's friends. Perhaps he had arranged the meeting for business. She didn't mind.

She rose early, bathed in the quiet sea. The water was clear, the beach deserted. She swam far out, dove beneath the waves, marveling at her white arms and soft flesh glowing underwater. She laughed, surfaced, swam back. Onshore, she saw the writer, the publishing director, and the district chairman in the villa yard.

The writer spotted her, waved, came down the slope.

"You're beautiful," he said. "You woke the sea earlier than usual."

"Thank you. Take a swim."

"No. Now that you've left it, the sea is cold again."

"Are you flirting with me?"

"No, praising beauty."

"But I hear it."

"Yes, but I speak for the sea. Since you stand beside it, you hear too."

They climbed the slope. She rinsed off; he met the chairman reading a newspaper.

"The Mỹ Hương gang's all caught," the chairman said.

The writer glanced at the headline—106 kilos of gold, 15 billion dong seized. He tossed the paper.
"First Đường Sơn Quán, now Mỹ Hương Just distractions from Eastern Europe."

"These are serious cases," the chairman replied.

"In advanced countries prostitution is legal, regulated. They prevent disease effectively. Here we ban and jail, yet prostitutes abound, diseases spread. So what does the Đường Sơn Quán case mean?"

"But officials were corrupt."

"Forget it. Did you lose money in Mỹ Hương perfumes?"

"No."

The director joined them, lively. The writer teased him about investing.

"This man's my friend, a genius," the director said. Wouldn't you agree, Phượng?"

"I do. And so are you."

"Right. From nothing, I built success."

"Success? He only cheated people," the chairman said.

"But not easily. Try it yourself."

They debated loudly, politics mixing with business.

Later, all went into the water—monk, writer, chairman, director, even Phi Mã. They played like children, splashing, clinging to a large float. Phi Mã pushed it away, swam with Phượng far out.

"Don't go too far," he cautioned.

"Leave those big shots with their float," she said.

"But if one falls, he'll drown."

"Then let him. Whoever doesn't belong to the sea will be swallowed by it."

They turned back. Indeed, the float drifted with the current. The writer panicked:

"It's drifting, Phượng!"

"Great! Write a poem!" she shouted.

They begged for help. Phượng teased them, demanding answers to sharp questions—about religion, literature, democracy—before pulling them in. Finally, she stood upright; the water barely reached her chest. The men realized they were near shore. They splashed clumsily, like a routed army.

*

That night, by the pool, they drank beer. Phượng, in bright dress, tanned skin, wild hair, looked like an African jungle orchid. The writer asked when she learned to swim. She said she never properly learned. The monk admitted he grew up in the mountains, no rivers or seas.

Phượng asked the district chairman:

"You lived in jungles and rivers for years during the revolution, why can't you swim?"

"Because I was a leader," he laughed. "Others ferried me across."

"But if ambushed, forced to dive, then what?"

He laughed louder, avoided the answer. Instead, he told a war story, how a courier once saved him during an ambush, shoving him into the river. He nearly drowned, dragged the boy down with him, until the courier knocked him out to save him. Years later, he met that courier again, in a circus. The boy had become a clown.

The monk coldly muttered:

"He was uneducated."

Phượng asked:

"Was it the same clown now performing at Tao Dan Park?"

"I don't know," the district chairman said.

"I've never been there. So what does he look like?"

"I'm not really sure," she replied, "because he was in disguise: a bright red clown nose, a mouth stretched all the way to his ears, rolling white eyes, and hair like a lion's mane."

The writer joined the conversation absentmindedly:

"I was on that Southwest border mission too, remember? A mixed delegation of the committee, the front, and some artists. I think that day I also watched the circus. His act was flat and cheap."

The monk said:

"But why would a guerrilla fighter become a clown?"

"Not clear," the chairman replied. "His background was a mess."

The writer asked:

"Why would they use someone with such an unclear background?"

Phượng turned to the writer:

"Do you really care about background that much? Normally I see you mocking people who obsess over it."

"That depends on the case."

"Not true," Phượng said. "You're very contradictory. Sometimes you say background doesn't matter, as long as the person has talent and enthusiasm. And now you criticize him for having a messy background."

The writer was still searching for a way to defend himself when two young men stepped from the darkness of the beach into the pool's light. It was Mã Long and Hùng.

"Sorry, uncles," Hùng bowed and said. "May I speak with Phượng for a moment?"

Phượng stood up and walked toward a coconut tree. Mã Long said:

"When are you going back to Saigon?"

"Tomorrow noon."

"Let me send a suitcase with you. Tomorrow night just take it to the usual place. We won't be back until Saturday."

"Why so late?"

"Waiting for the ship. Oh, and watch out for that Captain Tùng. Has he divorced his wife yet?"

"Maybe he already has."

Hung asked:

"Are you really thinking of marrying him?"

"That's my business. It's private."

"Alright then, go back to the table. Tomorrow morning go to Bãi Dâu and pick up the suitcase. Drive there alone."

The two young men disappeared back into the darkness.

When Phượng returned to her seat, she found everyone strangely pensive, distant, lost in thought. Oddly, that pleased her. She took out a cigarette, lit it, and quietly gazed at her family.

9.

The story of Captain Tùng divorcing his wife happened unexpectedly. Just when he was trying to find a way to start a quarrel, the opportunity came suddenly. Tùng went into a frenzy, yelling like a madman. At that moment even he didn't know if he was quarreling to get divorced or if he was regretting the loss.

"You're an ox. Your head is an ox's head. I've warned you time and again, why do you still defy me?"

"You reap what you sow. How much has this household been spending every month? Just two adults and one child, yet nearly a million đồng a month."

"What? Nearly a million?"

"Excuse me, just your cigarettes alone, two packs a day, that's already four thousand. Then coffee, gas, and oil. And how much do you spend on books?" (Vân pointed to the bookshelf.) "Look, books stacked like a mountain. Have you read a single one?"

Tùng slammed the table, shouting:

"Insolent! Do I have to report to you when I read? What about the books by my bedside?"

"Yes, you read, but just a few pages before falling asleep. As for Western books, you only look at the pictures."

"Don't try to change the subject." Tùng paced back and forth like a monkey in a cage. "You're trying to cover up your own fault, huh? You're greedy and stupid. Don't you understand how much profit that scammer could possibly make from those cheap perfumes to pay you fourteen percent interest per month? If you had any brains, you'd know it was a swindle. Why did you dare hand him ten million đồng?"

"But you never said that before. Every month I brought home the interest, and you spent it happily. You even praised him for doing good business."

"Never! I despise swindlers, market trash, the uneducated."

"And you're educated, are you? If I remember right, when you went into the jungle you only had a high school diploma. You think I don't know? You think you can fool me with this massive bookshelf? Sorry, but some of my black-market friends are engineers, high school teachers. They could teach you."

"Teach shit. If you think they're so good, then go take them. I've heard people say they've seen men giving you rides in Chợ Lớn three times—three different men, hugging you by the waist. That's something I didn't even want to mention."

Vân spat on the floor.

"Three times is too few. More like ten times. Does that sting? If you're so tough, divorce me. I'm praying for it."

Tùng burst out laughing:

"OK. Ready! Write the paper, write it quick! This afternoon we'll go to court."

Vân sat in the armchair, regaining her composure, smiling brightly.

"Give yourself five minutes to think. While you think, I'll get paper and pen. Think carefully. You know my nature—once I write, it's final."

She opened the desk drawer, pulled out paper and pen, and glanced at the clock.

"It's ten oh-five. You have five minutes to decide."

Tùng was silent, face stiff, wanting to tremble but not daring to.

"Scared?" Vân asked.

You bastard, Tùng cursed silently. Why are you afraid? Isn't this what you wanted? He shouted to drive away his hesitation:

"Scared of what! Write the petition!"

Vân looked at the clock.

"You've got fifteen seconds left."

"No need to wait. Write it!"

So Vân wrote. *"The Socialist Republic of Vietnam. Independence - Freedom - Happiness. Petition for Divorce. To whom it may concern..."* She finished in five minutes, signed her name, and handed the paper to Tùng.

"Sign it!"

He signed. At that moment, he wasn't afraid.

That whole afternoon, after submitting the petition to the court and returning home, Tùng thought of Phượng and felt happy. He rode Vân's old Honda through deserted streets, imagining a beautiful, prosperous future. He felt relieved that everything had gone just as he wished.

But the next morning, he began to be afraid. The first person he feared was Phượng's father. He had never broached the matter with the man. Would he agree?

Tùng went to work but came home an hour early and stopped by Phượng's house. Everyone was away. The housekeeper said Phượng and her father had gone to Vũng Tàu.

He went home. In the days that followed, Vân treated him with such cold composure that it frightened him even more. He tested the waters:

"The court set the date for the twelfth of this month."

"Uh-huh," Vân replied.

"Will you be busy that day?"

"No."

And she continued brushing their child's hair, getting the child ready for school.

On the fourth day, Tùng decided to meet Mr. Phi Mã.

"Hello, comrade," Mr. Phi Mã greeted cheerfully. "Come in, have some coffee."

They sat in the living room because the yard was already flooded with sunlight.

"Where's your La Dalat car? Why are you riding a motobike?"

"I sold it. Planned to buy a new one but haven't yet."

"Come by my salon, I'll find you a good car. Or do you want to look now?"

"No, sir..." Tùng stammered. "I came to tell you something."

"...?"

"I... I'm divorcing my wife."

"Oh? Why? What happened?"

"Many things, sir. We've been together over ten years but we're incompatible, always quarreling."

"Quarreling is normal in marriage. How serious can it be to divorce?"

"She's stubborn and sharp-tongued. The family atmosphere is always tense. Recently she lost me ten million đồng."

"Lost where?"

"The Mỹ Hương perfume scheme. I warned her many times, but she wouldn't listen."

Mr. Phi Mã said:

"Then even more reason not to divorce. The family is facing difficulty—you need unity to survive. And you should think about the meaning of marriage."

Tùng drained his coffee in silence.

"But sir, at first I felt pity for her. But when I asked for a divorce, she challenged me, seemed glad, in fact. We've already filed, next week we go to court. That's why I came to know your thoughts on Phượng's decision."

"What decision?"

"Because Phượng told me to divorce my wife, then she'd marry me. But I wanted to tell you... I think Phượng has... Here is her letter."

Mr. Phi Mã put on his glasses.

Anh Tùng,

At first I thought we were just having fun as friends. But now I realize I like you a lot. I don't like flowery words. Why live with that shrewish woman you described? What I promised you on our trip to Thủ Đức, I'll keep. Divorce quickly. After our wedding we'll go to France.

P.S. I'm ordering your car. The shipment arrives next month.

The letter was unsigned, but Mr. Phi Mã recognized his daughter's handwriting and tone. He set it on the table and pressed the intercom. Shortly, Phượng came down from upstairs, wearing a simple white dress that made her dazzlingly beautiful, completely unlike her usual streetwise look.

"Hello."

"Hello, Phượng," Tùng said quickly, snatching the letter into his pocket.

She sat beside her father, poured tea.

"Daughter" Mr. Phi Mã said, "I have a question."

She smiled:

"You're making me nervous, like I'm about to get married."

"Don't joke. Answer me: why have you kept your matter with Tùng from me?"

"I didn't hide anything. We're just friends."

"Then why did you write this letter?"

He looked around.

"Where is it?"

Tùng stammered miserably:

"You promised me..."

"Promised what? I forget things easily. What did I promise you?"

Humiliated and enraged, Tùng pulled the letter from his pocket and slapped it on the table.

Phượng laughed, wrapped her arm around her father's shoulders, stroked the graying hair at his nape.

"Oh right, I remember. That was when I was crazy. I often go crazy like that. Why keep it? I thought you'd thrown it away."

She picked it up, read it aloud while laughing, then handed it to her father.

"See, Dad? Pure madness."

Mr. Phi Mã stayed silent, looking uneasily at the young man across from him, face pale with anger. Suddenly, Phượng grew serious:

"Sorry, Tùng. I didn't mean to mock you. I just get fits of madness. Don't be angry."

Tùng shot up, shouting:

"You mad? You just wanted to humiliate me! Never in my life have I been disgraced like this, disgraced by a cheap junkie girl. But don't be smug. Remember, I am a police officer!"

"Calm down," Mr. Phi Mã said, raising his hand. "Sit down. What are you doing?"

"Let him talk, Dad," Phượng said. "He's already lost. The more he talks, the worse he loses. I wasn't mocking him. I only wanted to let him reveal his true nature. And now I'll judge. Right now I'm the chief investigator, not him."

Tùng shook with rage, the muscles of his eyelids and upper lip twitching pathetically. Before Mr. Phi Mã could ease the tension, Tùng suddenly lunged forward, grabbed the letter.

"I'll keep this as evidence."

"Evidence of what?" Phượng laughed. "That I seduced you? Or will you take it home to show your wife?"

Tùng stormed out.

But the farce wasn't over.

He sped home, imagining himself bursting through the door, falling to his knees before his wife, begging forgiveness. But when the door opened, the room was changed. Bedding rolled up, clothes gone. On the table, a letter:

Anh Tùng,

While waiting for the court, our child and I will stay with my mother. Don't waste time looking.

Tùng cursed and collapsed on the floor, gasping. The next morning he bought a ticket to his wife's hometown in Sa Đéc. But she hadn't gone there. Her parents worried, not knowing what had happened. Tùng explained it was just a quarrel over the Mỹ Hương affair. Then he returned to Sài Gòn, wondering where his wife and child had gone.

The day before the court date, Vân came back with the child.

Tùng put on a pitiful face.

"Where were you? I searched everywhere these past days."

"My child and I went out. Why should you care?"

"I want to apologize. It was just anger. I was stupid to insult you."

He knelt, trying to embrace her waist, but she pulled away, laughing coldly.

"Don't. You're not at fault. I also want the divorce. I've wanted it for a long time, not just because of what happened."

"But I can't live without you."

"Yes, you can. Don't be so pessimistic."

"Before, I thought I could live without you. But this past week, apart from you, I see I cannot."

"I'm the opposite. Before, I thought I could endure you, live life with you. But this past week I've realized I absolutely cannot. I must leave you. Please set me free. Look at me. My heart is cold, indifferent. Never have I felt so light, so at peace."

If only I could cry now, Tùng thought, *even a single tear. But I can't, though I'm miserable and humiliated.*

"Vân! Don't be angry so long. I haven't committed any great crime."

"It's not about crime."

"Then what?"

"Your personality—or rather, your nature. For more than ten years I've suffered from your arrogance. My friends, my parents, my siblings—all can't stand it. Everyone asks: 'What's so special about him that he acts so haughty?' And they shun me. Then all the petty things at home: I turn on the TV without a cotton ball, you scold me; I put warm water in the freezer, you're afraid I'll break the fridge. Do you remember the time you hit me because I forgot to take a birth control pill? You said that proved I didn't care about intimacy with you. But I was exhausted after work—washing diapers, mixing milk, rocking the baby—while you sat like a boss, sipping coffee and smoking, and forced me to remember the pill every night so you wouldn't 'waste' an evening. That was all about you, never about me. Honestly, ten years of that was enough. Now let me be free. I'm not jealous of Phượng, Mr. Phi Mã's daughter. In fact, I'm glad for you. Go live with her. Otherwise, my child and I will go."

Tùng sat frozen. He had no words left. Only after a long time did he stand.

"But in court I'll ask for a trial separation."

"Do as you like," Vân said firmly. "No matter what the court decides, I will not live with you again. At worst, I'll move in with my mother."

With that, she turned on the music and took her child to bathe.

10.

The Toyota 800 had just turned onto Tran Hung Dao Street when Phượng realized they were being followed. Their pursuers were four plainclothes criminal police officers riding black CD 90s. Mã Long accelerated, heading straight toward Sai Gon.

"At the Ben Thanh roundabout, park at the South Gate. Phượng and I will jump out and run into the market while you drive straight down Nguyen Trai," he instructed.

The clock atop Ben Thanh Market showed 8:10 p.m. The Toyota 800 screeched to a stop in front of the South Gate. Hùng and Phượng leapt out. Phượng carried the small suitcase while Hùng followed close behind to cover her. The market was already closed, but they slipped through the crowd of pedestrians and disappeared into the shadows of Phan Boi Chau Street.

The two CD 90s tried to cross the road, but the heavy traffic coming from Le Loi blocked them in the middle of the street. The two plainclothes officers on the back seats had to give chase on foot, while Phượng and Hùng mounted a waiting Cub and sped off toward Ta Thu Thau.

The two CD 90s soon caught up. The chase unfolded in full view of passersby. Clothing shops preparing to close became chaotic; people poured into the street, crowding it completely.

Hùng swerved onto Nguyen Trung Truc Street. The two CD bikes followed, firing several warning shots into the air. At Nguyen Du, Hùng turned left and gunned the throttle.

Phượng urged him:

"Try to make it to Cach Mang Thang Tam. There are lots of music venues there—we can ditch the bike and vanish into the crowd."

Hùng blared the horn, weaving recklessly at top speed. But near the junction of Cach Mang Thang Tam, they collided with an oncoming Cub without headlights. Hùng braked hard, the bike skidded sideways onto the sidewalk, and both crashed to the ground.

The two CD 90s arrived. Hùng, injured in the leg, couldn't run and was caught. Phượng dashed into the crowd, clutching her suitcase. The police blew their whistles, chasing her. At that moment, a performance had just ended, and the theatergoers filled the street. Phượng melted into the throng.

But she didn't dare break onto the main road. She scaled an iron fence, slipped into the yard of a comedy theater, then crossed another crowd and climbed over two more fences.

Police whistles shrilled behind her. Glancing back, she saw the crowd outside the comedy theater in disarray. She decided to run straight into the Labor Culture House. Ahead of her shone a blaze of lights—it was the circus. Phượng rushed toward it. But since a show was underway, the outer yard was empty. She ran behind the canvas tent and hid in a bush next to the stone bench where the clown used to sit and drink water.

By then the four officers had reached the tennis courts, their flashlights sweeping the paths by the pool.

Phượng was about to move when a shadow emerged from the circus tent. It was the clown. She suddenly stepped out of the bushes, startling him.

"Who's there?" he asked.

"It's Phượng. Do you remember me?"

The clown grinned, making his painted face look grotesque.

"Lost your watch again?"

Phượng grabbed his wrist, speaking quickly:

"The police are after me. Please save me."

The clown stared, thinking she was joking. Just then three gunshots cracked, flashlight beams flickered, and the four policemen circled around the pavilion.

"They're after me," Phượng said. "Take me away."

The clown listened for a moment, then said:

"Wait here."

He went to fetch his motorbike. Thirty seconds later, the two of them roared out of the Labor Culture House grounds, reaching Huyen Tran Cong Chua Street.

The clown's old Suzuki sputtered and rattled all the way past the Sai Gon Bridge. It was nearly 10 p.m. But a little further on, the bike broke down. He pulled the spark plug to scrape it, but it still wouldn't start.

"What a piece of junk!" Phượng snapped. "Burn it already."

"Burn it then," the clown said, handing her his lighter.

Only now did Phượng notice he was still in full makeup. Sweat had smeared the greasepaint and powder into a hideous mask.

"Wipe your face," she said.

"No need," he replied. "I've got to fix the bike first."

But Phượng pulled a pistol from her waistband. She stood in the middle of the road, waiting.

Just then a middle-aged man rode up on a Honda 67 from Sai Gon. Phượng spread her arms to block him.

"Get off the bike!" she shouted, aiming at his chest. "Yell and I'll shoot."

The man looked ready to resist, but when he saw the ghastly clown looming, he panicked and fled.

The clown seemed delighted, laughing loudly. He flicked his lighter, ripped out the Suzuki's fuel line, and set it ablaze.

They mounted the stolen Honda. Suddenly Phượng said:

"Follow that man."

"You mean to kill him?"

"Don't ask."

The clown turned the bike around, forcing the man to the curb. Seeing the clown with his red nose chasing him, the man folded his hands in terror.

"Please spare me."

Phượng said:

"Don't be afraid. Keep this suitcase. Sell it, and you'll have enough for a new bike."

She tossed the suitcase before the trembling man, then climbed back onto the Honda.

They sped off toward Bien Hoa.

The clown drove fast, laughing uproariously.

"I like your style," he said.

Phượng sighed with relief. The cool wind eased her nerves.

"You're reckless too. So where do we go now?"

"I was about to ask you that."

"I don't know."

"Neither do I. But we'll just ride until the gas runs out."

Phượng asked:

"Do you have any friends with a farm?"

"Yes. But far away—in Long Khanh."

"Check the tank."

He dipped his finger into the fuel. It was still full.

"If you want, we've got enough to get there."

"I'd like that."

"So you're running away for good?"

"Yes."

"But what did you do to get chased like this?"

"Robbery."

"You need money that badly?"

"No."

"Then why rob?"

Phượng laughed.

"Do you know what was in that suitcase?"

"Dollars, I guess?"

"Opium. I'm a smuggler. There are three in our gang. One got caught back there. The suitcase had five kilos of opium."

"Why'd you leave it behind?"

"Because I don't need money. I just like thrills. But my friends, they love getting rich. What about you? Do you crave wealth?"

The clown shook his head.

"Sadly, my trade doesn't make money. Being a clown is just for fun."

"So now you're leaving the circus to go with me?"

"If I hadn't met you tonight, I would've left someday anyway. I've changed my life a dozen times already."

"They say you once fought in the resistance war, is that true?"

"Who says so?"

"The district chairman. He's my father's friend. He said once you and he were ambushed crossing a river and your boat sank."

"Maybe."

"And the writer and the monk? They said they met you on a trip to the Southwest border. True?"

The clown burst out laughing, slowing the bike.

"So you know those guys too? What does your father do?"

"Roughly speaking, he's a businessman. But not an official. He plays tennis with those people. They don't seem to like you much, though."

"They live fake lives. Fake lives in a fake society. Don't you feel that, hanging around them?"

"Sometimes I feel almost everyone around me lives falsely. Yet they endure it their whole lives, even take pride in it. Like that publishing director—also my father's friend. He colluded with the writer, pushing him to churn out all sorts of books: anti-corruption stories, renovation stories, martial arts stories... He funded the print runs, got rich. With too much money, he gambled, chased women, drank every night. Recently he resigned and declared: 'I'll quit the Party, join a new Party, become a leader.' Do you think he'll succeed?"

"Why not? People like that usually do."

They passed through a dense, shadowy rubber forest and reached a village dimly lit by scattered lamps. Phượng checked her watch.

"Almost midnight. We should find somewhere to rest till morning. I'm scared riding like this."

"Don't worry," the clown said. "We're almost there. Just seven kilometers more."

"But slow down. I feel cold."

He kept the speed at thirty kilometers an hour, passed through two more rubber groves, and turned onto a side path. Luckily his headlight was bright enough to cut through the gloom. Soon dogs barked, and a faint light appeared through the low trees. He stopped in front of a thatched hut. The dogs barked furiously. The clown stood by the bike, Phượng hiding behind him. After a while there were noises inside, then a small door opened.

"Who's there?"

The dogs, recognizing a familiar scent, ran joyfully to the clown.

"Anh Hai, is that you?" the clown called.

"It's me. Who's that?"

"The clown here, Anh Hai."

"Well well, what brings you here so late? Being chased by soldiers?"

The clown laughed loudly.

"Maybe so. This is my friend."

Phượng stepped into the light, greeting the man.

"You must be surprised."

The man gave a dry, calm laugh.

"Not at all, miss. He's always appeared and vanished like a ghost."

He set an oil lamp on the table. His arms were big, dark, and hairy like an ape's. He pointed to a coarse hammock.

"Lie down and rest here. Tomorrow we'll talk."

Then he pulled the clown by the arm and led him out back.

11.

It was the first time in her life that Phượng awoke to the strange silence of a radiant morning. She opened her eyes and immediately saw that silence. It stretched vast and boundless, sometimes near, sometimes far, caressing the air—reminded only by the gentle rustle of the wind, the sound of a dry leaf falling onto the thatched roof, or the lonely call of a small bird in the corner of the garden.

The sunlight was fresh, as if it had just flown through a shower of rain to reach her. The silence made Phượng feel awake yet still dreamy, as though she were in a magical vision.

When a spider dropped from the roof beam right in front of her, Phượng startled and sat up. Her sandals were still neatly on the ground. She went down to the kitchen but saw no one; it seemed there was no sound of people in the garden either.

Phượng walked to the front yard and sat under a jackfruit tree. It was still young but lush with thick branches, heavy with fruit hanging low. She tilted her head back to look at the canopy—it spread like an umbrella above her. A large, round fruit dangled right before her, within arm's reach. Suddenly there was a bird's song, then silence. She sat down on a bamboo bed next to the embers of a fire long gone out.

The spotted dog from the garden came in, wagging its tail halfheartedly. Phượng stroked its head, it lifted its snout, then lay down beside her leather sandals.

The dense orchard before her was an entirely new world. Tall trees, wide canopies, and shadows covered the ground. The path between the trees was shaded, dappled with sunlight, making the garden seem endless, mysterious, and alluring.

Phượng gazed into the orchard, not knowing where it would lead. It felt vast like a forest, and the thatched hut she sat in seemed only a tiny bird's nest, completely alone. She looked around, trying to recall the trail that the clown had brought her along last night, but she was clueless. It felt as though she had been abandoned here, left with demons, wild beasts, and snakes.

Yet that fear quickly faded when a sweet fragrance of ripe fruit drifted to her. It was an unusual scent, sometimes faint, sometimes strong.

Phượng stood up and walked cautiously, like a lost child in the forest. The fragrance drew her on. The further she went, the stronger the scent became, and when she heard the sound of trickling water, it grew intoxicating. She found herself surrounded by a forest of mit-tố-nữ trees, heavy with fruit. She touched one hanging before her, and it fell right into her hand, leaving her bewildered.

Just then came the sound of footsteps rustling on the leaves.

A man appeared on the path, carrying a cluster of ripe red fruit.

At first she thought it was the clown, but as he came closer, she saw it was a man in his thirties, with thick eyebrows and a somber gaze tinged with melancholy. Something in that look stirred a memory in Phượng.

She stared at him, but her expression did not surprise him. He handed her the cluster of fruit. She took it mechanically, her eyes fixed on his face. His hair was short, eyebrows thick, eyes straight and lively, a faint mustache, a confident smile with a touch of irony.

Is this the clown's real face? she thought, then quickly dismissed the idea. She was sure she had seen this face before, long ago.

"Do you like this fruit?" he asked.

"What kind of fruit is it?" Phượng whispered.

"I don't know either. It's a wild fruit from the forest—can't be eaten. I just thought it looked pretty, so I picked it."

They walked along the sun-dappled path.

"Is this your garden?" she asked.

"No. It belongs to a friend of mine."

"You're not surprised to see me here?"

"No. Because I've known you for a long time."

"Since when?"

They looked at each other.

"A long time ago."

Phượng pondered, then suddenly grabbed his hand.

"I remember now! I once wanted to go to Duyên Hải to find you."

"For what?"

"To give you some money. After that time I met you there, I kept wondering why someone like you had to be just a commune secretary. I felt sorry for you."

"You really thought that?"

"Yes. You seemed more like a poor hippy than a secretary. The way you spoke to that big official was so hesitant. I liked it. Almost the whole time I was there, I only noticed you among that noisy crowd of cadres."

"I was going to say the same. I knew you were sitting in that cramped corner of the

Committee office, your head resting against the bamboo wall."

Phượng let go of his hand without embarrassment and raised the fruit cluster to her nose, but it had no scent. They wandered for a long while and still hadn't reached the end of the orchard, perhaps only circling the paths.

"You're no longer a secretary?" she asked.

"No. They fired me."

"Who? That official?"

"Could be."

"When did you come to live here?"

"Last night."

Phượng grabbed his wrist again, this time tightly, as if interrogating him.

"Last night?"

"Yes. Late at night. I came here with a girl on a stolen bike."

"Oh my God!" Phượng burst out laughing. "You really are the clown. But was that a promotion or a demotion?"

"Neither. Just a career change."

"Liar. But never mind. At least when I see you clowning on stage, I feel less sorry than when you had to receive that official."

"What was pitiful about that day?"

"Actually, you behaved well that day. But *because* it was too good, I felt sorry that someone like you had to live under another's power."

The clown laughed.

"So you wanted to give me money?"

"Yes. But let me ask you this: Why did you choose to be a clown?"

"Because it's easy. Just paint your face, wear a skirt, and people laugh."

"And now, leaving that job to wander with me, do you regret it?"

"Yes."

"What do you regret?" Phượng asked.

"The money you intended to give me."

Phượng laughed until she bent over. They returned to the thatched hut.

"I'm glad to see you happy," the clown said.

"But if I stay here too long, I'll get bored," Phượng replied.

"So if you're thrown into life outside, how will you survive?" he asked.

"I've never worried about money. Many times I've wanted to leave home and wander, but my pockets had to be full. So how do we get money?"

"For example, by doing tricks of illusion," he said.

"Where did you learn that?"

"Back in the forest. Friends taught me."

"And the watch-stealing trick?"

"I made that up myself."

"Teach me."

"If so, it'll take time. For now, let's find something to eat."

They went to the kitchen. The Honda 67 was parked there.

"That's a good bike," Phượng said. "But we'll need to change the license plate."

"When we leave, we'll change it."

They rummaged for cold rice to eat. In the pen were some ripe mangoes, though still hard. The clown picked one and gave it to Phượng, then asked:

"Where's your gun?"

Phượng suddenly remembered. She went to the tree hollow near the hammock, pulled out the Colt 45, and handed it to him.

"I'll keep it," he said. "We'll need it someday."

12.

The flea market was set up right in the village path, and the clown parked his bike at the entrance. Phượng said:

"Wait here for me."

The market was sparse. Baskets of fruit, peanuts, mung beans, and stalls selling wild meat lined both sides of the road. The local people dressed sloppily, like farm workers. Most wore old, faded army shirts or work jackets. Phượng went all the way to the end of the market but still didn't find what she wanted to buy. When she turned back, she saw the clown holding a small monkey in his arms.

"Does it bite?" Phượng asked.

"Make friends with it."

Phượng picked up the little monkey and remembered the bear she had at home.

The clown asked:

"Did you find what you needed?"

Phượng shook her head.

He drove the girl deeper into town. Shops stood unevenly, with thatched roofs mixed with corrugated iron, low forest trees left standing with red dust clinging to their leaves, noodle shops blaring music. The farmers sitting in the shops all turned to look at the two of them. A herd of goats crossed, blocking the bike, forcing the clown to stop and wait.

Phượng said:

"I like these lonely little towns. They're wild and savage. I like meeting these mixed people who gather here from everywhere. Look at them drinking coffee."

They puffed on cigarettes, wore tattered jeans patched in many places. Their beards were scraggly, hair long and sunburnt.

"They look like Gypsies," Phượng said.

"They're just like us," the clown replied. "People on the run. Criminals. Drug smugglers, like you."

"Too bad," Phượng said, "I'm only an amateur smuggler."

"You're a bomb," the clown said, "wanting to explode just to show off."

Phượng slapped his shoulder, told him to stop. She ran into a general store and bought a set of pajamas and some cheap underwear.

"I don't want to go back yet," Phượng said. "Let's see what's over there in those hills?"

The bike carried them on. The sky was bright but cloudy. A slope of red earth slanted gently down to a green patch of crops.

"When you were little," Phượng asked, "did you live in the countryside or the city?"

"I lived in this village."

"Really? Then are there any sights around here?"

"I'll take you to an old temple. The scenery there is very secluded."

The clown turned onto a dirt road cutting through the fields. The temple wasn't far from town, tucked inside thick trees. It was hidden within a large rock cave; even its curved roof seemed naturally formed by the random arrangement of stones. Yet it wasn't dark or damp. Holes in the cliffs let in light and cool breezes.

As soon as they stepped inside, they heard the steady, mournful sound of a wooden fish. A monk sat with his back to the door, his bald head slightly bowed.

The clown whistled; the sound echoed through the stone walls.

"Why are you making noise?" Phượng said.

The clown laughed.

"Don't worry. He's deaf."

He pulled a firecracker from his pocket, lit it, and tossed it right behind the monk. It exploded.

Only then did the monk turn around.

It was Lỗ Trí Thâm from the *Water Margin*. But this master stroked his scraggly beard, raised his brows, and pressed his palms together to bow to the clown.

"Uncle Master!" Lỗ Trí Thâm said. "Have you grown tired of the dust of the world and come here?"

"Tired? Not at all," the clown said. "Life is fun."

"What's fun about life?"

"Life is chaotic. Don't you listen to the radio?"

"No. I don't read newspapers either."

"Then you don't know what's happening in Eastern Europe?"

"What about Eastern Europe?"

"They shot Ceaușescu."

Lỗ Trí Thâm rubbed his bald head with his massive hand.

"Who's that? A drug smuggler?"

The clown lit another small firecracker with his cigarette and tossed it. After it popped, he said:

"If you don't know, I'm not telling. But do you know a man named Nguyễn Văn Mười Ba?"

Lỗ Trí Thâm burst out laughing.

"That one, this poor monk knows."

That reply surprised Phượng. She asked:

"How do you know him?"

"This poor monk is a man of religion, I know nothing of money," Lỗ Trí Thâm said.

He only stroked his beard and smiled without answering further. At that moment, five or six women, some old, some middle-aged, some young, rushed out from behind the temple.

"What exploded, Master?"

"My honored guests" Lỗ Trí Thâm said. "Firecrackers in celebration. Prepare a vegetarian meal for them."

The nuns obeyed but cast wary glances at Phượng.

The clown stopped them:

"No need, we're leaving now."

"Why so soon?" the monk asked.

"Master, we still have many things to do."

He pulled Phượng outside. There was giggling among the nuns peeking from behind the stone walls.

Outside, Phượng asked:

"Who were those women?"

"They're from town. His wives."

"Why so strange?"

I think it's perfectly normal. I was the one who discovered his genius."

"What genius?"

"Master Lỗ Trí Thâm, who else?"

And the clown began telling her the story of how he first met the monk...

"Right after the *liberation*, before returning to Duyen Hai, I had been chairman here. One night, coming back from a meeting, I passed through a cassava field and heard groans. I drew his pistol and crept through the dark rows of cassava toward the sound. It turned out to be a couple making love."

Phượng asked:

"Why did you interrupt their fun like that?"

"I didn't interrupt. At first I thought someone was injured, because right after the liberation the security situation was very complicated. When I realized it was just a couple, I laughed and asked: Do you need my help? I only said it as a joke. Unexpectedly, the man laughed and said: No, we're done. Aren't you the commune chairman? I've heard people say you're quite the player, and it seems they were right. I was surprised that someone caught red-handed could still respond so confidently. So I asked: Where are you from, friend? The man and woman had already dressed by then. The man struck a match to light his cigarette. The flare revealed a face full of beard and a bald head. His smile delighted me, it was confident, innocent, and oddly charming. I exclaimed: Oh, Master! I'd heard of you back in the jungle. Your reputation is well deserved. And that's how we became close friends. Later, during drinking parties in the temple, the master confessed he had twelve wives, all of them nuns and temple women serving there."

Phượng said:

"He's too clever."

The clown replied:

"Not clever. He was just doing charity for the world. I love such people."

He pushed the Honda 67 down a trail and kicked the engine to life.

Phượng climbed on behind him. She asked:

"Why do you like provoking people?"

"Because I'm a clown."

"But you're only a clown on stage."

The clown laughed loudly:

"I was born to be a clown, just as others are born to be monks, doctors, writers, or politicians."

Phượng asked:

"So even in your mother's womb you were already a clown?"

"Maybe. My mother said when I was born, my legs came out first. Isn't that a clown's trick?"

"Not necessarily," Phượng said. "Maybe you were cowardly, afraid of the rats biting you, so you sent your legs first to test the waters."

The clown laughed, squeezed Phượng's knee hard:

"Alright, that must be it. Afraid of rats. Even now, at thirty-four, I'm still afraid of rats."

"But when you were in school you must have been well-behaved?"

"No. I was terrible at studying, hardly ever learned my lessons."

"Loved cockfighting, didn't you?"

"No. I only started learning A.B.C. at ten. At twelve, I went through a terrifying crisis."

"Girl-crazy, right?"

"No. It began with the death of a neighbor. He was very old. Every day he collected clay from the fields to mold little birds, cutting paper wings and tails, using beads for eyes. His parrots were all made of clay and hollow inside, with a bamboo whistle inserted in the belly. He hung those toys on a small straw stick and wandered the village, blowing into the bird bellies like a trumpet. At twelve I was fascinated by them. I was close to the old man. Then one day he suddenly died. My God, the face of death was horrible: eye sockets and cheeks sunken, skin yellow as turmeric, legs stiff as wood. That death planted not only fear but a crushing despair in me. Just yesterday he'd laughed and talked, puffing into the parrot belly, and suddenly he was inert, like stone, like dust, like dry wood. I cried and asked my father: Daddy, the old man died, where did he go? Father answered coldly: Dead is the end. Nowhere to go. Will I die too? He stammered, staring at the twelve-year-old in shock. At last he said: Everyone must die, son."

I burst into tears. I still remember vividly the crushing loneliness I felt from that answer. The despair cut me off from innocence and childhood joys, like a knife. That was the cruelest, most unexpected blow death ever dealt me. It left a wound that never healed, an eternal obsession haunting me even in my happiest moments."

Phượng asked:

"But when did you get past that gloom?"

"Puberty, perhaps. (He laughed, glancing back at Phượng's red lips.) When I started loving girls, everything else was swept away."

"Which girl bewitched you so badly?"

"Not a girl, but a married woman, older than my sister. I was eighteen then, in eleventh grade. I often studied with a classmate, the youngest in his family. The woman was already mature, with husband and children. I was a skinny kid, not attractive, yet whenever I sat or stood somewhere she'd come near. At first I didn't notice, but her gestures repeated so often that I grew suspicious. Then she became bolder, laying her hand on my thigh, slapping my cheek playfully, stroking my hair. She teased and lured, quietly enticing me. She became my heaven, my longing. But it was all silent, a secret hot war.

"One day I came by and she was alone at home. She showed me a new photo of herself. Just an ordinary photo. I thought: an old woman being vain. I didn't like the photo. In person she wasn't beautiful either, but flesh and blood, warm, soft, breathing heavily. In person it was different. As I looked at the photo, she came up from behind, arms reaching around, pretending to point at it. Her tongue faltered, my limbs weakened. Suddenly she pressed against me. Her large, soft breasts crushed into my back, milk spurting onto my shirt. Her lower body burned against my hips. I thought I'd burst like an over-inflated balloon. The photo slipped from my hands. Her hot mouth brushed my ear, whispering deadly words: 'Turn around!'

"I turned. Top and bottom fit perfectly. She clutched me tight. Burning. Urgent. I was smothered, crushed, drowned on the tiled floor. And all of it happened in heaven."

Phượng suddenly staggered off the bike, collapsing into the grass. The clown stopped, rushed over:

"What's wrong?"

"Your story was too much. I felt weak."

He lifted her and saw a fresh streak of blood trickling down her forehead, like a worm crawling along her nose. He took out his handkerchief to wipe it, but Phượng pushed him away.

"Leave it."

"Does it hurt?" he asked.

"No. It calmed me down. Go on, this story is somehow tied to my father's monk friend, isn't it?"

"Yes," he said. "But let me finish this first love of mine. A week later she called me over. I said I was afraid. Her husband was a captain in the field police, but she told me no one would be home that day. I skipped class and came. She dragged me into the bathroom, turned the shower on full blast, and toyed with me like a cat with a mouse. I was bold, but she was ten times bolder. She bit, clawed, devoured me like a wolf. Water poured down like rain. I knelt, face up. Her long, sagging breasts swung against my cheeks, pressed into my face. Water streamed into her nipples and poured into my mouth. Just then came a knock on the bathroom door. Before we could react, the door was kicked open. The captain, her husband, stood there, facing the two of us naked. If you were her, how would you react?"

Phượng said:

"If I truly loved you and hated my husband, I'd tell him."

"Or would you kneel and beg him for forgiveness?"

"Maybe, if you were just a fling."

The clown laughed easily, tossed a stone into the bushes:

"All our guesses are wrong. That woman acted differently."

"How?" Phượng asked.

"She collapsed, head on the tub, crying: 'Darling, this bastard raped me!' The captain was calm. He asked: 'But how did he get into the bathroom?' She sobbed: 'No one was home, so I bathed without locking the door. He slipped in, locked it, and shoved me into the tub.'

Her words stunned me. It was like seeing the dead face of that old toy-seller again. Shock and horror. Just moments ago she'd been laughing, tender, and suddenly she was something else entirely. How much like death is betrayal! I became infamous in the city for that bizarre 'rape.' I was sentenced to two years in prison. That was the gift of my first love. Perhaps the vilest first love on the planet, leaving me utterly disillusioned with humanity.Two years later, when I got out, I heard she had left the captain for a Black American GI. People whispered the captain was impotent. And it seemed true. I pitied him. One day I decided to visit, to tell him the truth about that day, to comfort him, to urge him to forget her. But he was proud. He neither believed me nor admitted his impotence. He drew his gun and shot me. The bullet pierced my side, broke a rib, but I survived. After leaving the hospital, weary, I returned to my hometown, where no one knew my scandals. I worked the fields and mingled with guerrillas."

Phượng asked:

"So when did you meet the district chairman?"

"Four years later, just after Tết Mậu Thân Offensive."

"And the monk?"

"The monk was that very captain. His going into monkhood only confirmed his impotence."

"But why did he become a monk?"

"Perhaps to avoid re-education camp."

*

At that moment they both fell silent, hearing footsteps. Not on the trail, but rustling through thick cassava.

"Don't be sad," a man's voice said. "Everyone has their fate. Consider it three million lost, but disaster avoided."

"What disaster? Losing three million is disaster enough" a woman wept.

"But many lost ten times more. An old retiree put all his savings in and lost everything. Worst are treasurers who poured in tens of millions. Gone."

"Didn't the boss flee abroad with his family?"

"Not fleeing. He left openly, by plane, escorted to the airport, big shots seeing him off. He's smarter than Nguyen Van Muoi Ba."

"I heard there's a blind man too. How could a blind man run a company?"

"That's the marvel. He wasn't just recently blind, he's been blind since birth. He never knew money, never knew green from red, square from round, never saw a face, never read a word. Yet they appointed him director. When he went bankrupt, they said the law doesn't punish the blind, so he carried on happily. At home, women did his nails, one young wife on the left, one maid on the right, a beer in hand, dark glasses on his eyes. Outside, crowds swarmed like flies demanding withdrawals, crying, cursing, blocking traffic, police whistles shrilling, sweat pouring."

The group, talking, passed by the clown and Phượng but, hidden by bushes, didn't see them.

Phượng asked:

"In such remote places, people still send money to savings banks in Saigon?"

"They had branches everywhere," the clown said.

He rolled the bike back to Phượng, kicked the engine, and they returned to the main road toward the orchard.

A ward policeman sat waiting on a bamboo bed outside. He was chatting casually with the orchard owner, not tense. The clown drove straight into the yard, parked by a jackfruit tree.

"Hello," the clown said.

The policeman nodded. Without preamble he said:

"You two have stayed here nearly a week without registering."

The clown replied:

"We'll leave soon."

"Even one night requires registration. Where are you from?"

"Bien Hoa," Phượng answered.

The policeman said:

"Please understand. Society is complicated now." (He flipped through a newspaper.) "Fraud everywhere, killings, smuggling. Recently in the city they busted a big smuggling ring, arrested everyone, only the daughter of tycoon Phi Mã escaped. Look here."

The clown glanced at the paper, but what caught his eye wasn't the escape of Phi Ma's daughter, but news of the district chairman's involvement in the blind tycoon scandal. He handed the paper to Phượng, but she skimmed it indifferently, as if uninterested.

The clown opened a pack of Jet, offered the policeman a cigarette, invited him for drinks that evening. The policeman gladly accepted. When he left, the clown walked him out, chatting cheerfully, so much that the man forgot to take back his paper.

But that evening's drinking never happened. Instead of the lone ward policeman, an armed squad appeared in the orchard. Luckily, at that moment the clown and Phượng were picking ripe sapodillas. The dogs barked, warning them. The clown told Phượng to hide in the bushes while he slipped into the kitchen, wheeled out the Honda 67, tore a hole in the fence, sped across cassava fields, and burst onto the highway.

13.

A crowd gathered around a corner of the market. The market was as shabby as the poor, ramshackle little town itself. In this coastal town, May came with howling winds and stormy rains. The sea was rough, the water muddy, and the waves roared through the night. In the morning, the sun rose sluggishly, sometimes buried in the clouds, making the town drowsy and lazy. After seven o'clock, only a single bus left the station with just a handful of passengers. An old woman selling bread cried her wares like a long-drawn-out lament, while dogs barked absently and out of tune in the deserted streets. Only the early market had a little bustle.

The clown performed magic tricks on the church steps. He had nothing but a crimson veil, a paper bowler hat made from cigarette cartons, a little stick, some ping-pong balls, and a deck of cards. Yet he managed to draw a crowd. On her first appearance before the public, Phượng felt shy, but the clown was so natural, lively, and quick that she grew more confident. She only helped with trivial things—handing him the stick, picking up a ball that fell to the ground, or lighting his cigarette. Everything else the clown did himself. By the fourth day, Phượng could already accompany herself on the guitar and sing. But her voice was too husky, more suited to a cabaret than a street corner, and the crowd didn't care much for her singing. Still, her presence made the clown's act less monotonous. She gave the audience a breather, and gave the clown time to pick up the coins that fell on the ground.

The clown walked on his hands, so his oversized pants kept slipping down, exposing his bony shins. Afterward, Phượng thought of tying his pant legs with rubber bands, and thanks to that, he could stand on his hands comfortably. The audience was delighted and laughed. Phượng cried. Because Phượng knew the man called the clown. But those tears were held back many times, and later they no longer came. Everything became ordinary.

By afternoon the two of them earned five thousand đồng, and they cooked their meal in a sheltered corner by the old cathedral. They usually returned after the evening service, when the devout had already gone home and the church stood empty. The bell sounds dissolved into the sea wind; the gray bell tower and the gray cathedral stood solitary on the desolate shore, filled with smoky waves. The sea was still rough, the strong wind blew, whipping at their little fire. They huddled together in the cold afternoon. The flame kept flickering, yellow and weak. The sea was vast and gray. The black reefs stood mute. The sea had been battering them for a million years but was never sated. The sea was never calm when they came here. They ate under the church eaves and drank bitter strong tea in the dark. That was the clown's old habit from the resistance war. Phượng couldn't drink at first, but she tried. It wasn't so hard after all. She just drank, and fought off the drowsiness.

When night fell over the furious sea, their little dark corner by the church became warm and cozy. They sat close together, backs against the mossy wall, sharing the same cigarette. Sometimes Phượng sang, without guitar, because it was too cold and the sea wind blew spray into their faces. But that was the fun of it. Phượng often forgot the lyrics, and then she giggled, while the clown carried on, sounding like a drake, raspy like a wooden horn. But the clown forgot even worse than she did—just humming "i... i..." like a child. They kissed and made love on the cold stone ground. Sleep came, lasting until midnight, sometimes until dawn when the clown rose, coughing dryly and waking Phượng.

The clown asked:

"Do you like living with me like this?"

"Very much."

"We're so poor. Who knows when we'll buy a yacht."

"We'll buy a horse cart instead."

"But even a horse isn't easy to get—unless we steal one."

"Why don't you teach me to steal watches?"

"In time."

"Why not now?"

"Because the people here are poor. All their watches are cheap, not worth taking. I'll take you to the kingdom of King Solomon, or to an Arab kingdom, and we'll steal golden watches studded with diamonds."

"When will we go to that kingdom?"

"When we're hunted down here."

Lightning flashed on the horizon, lighting the sea for an instant before darkness returned. They said no more. They made love again and slept until just before the morning service. Sometimes they overslept and had to hurriedly pack their things before heading back to the market.

They didn't know what day it was, only that the market seemed busier than usual, filled with flowers and birds for sale. Cages crammed with flocks of sparrows, finches, and rice birds chattered noisily. Wealthy, well-dressed women came early to buy hundreds of these birds and release them in front of the market, clasping their hands in prayer. Phượng was astonished:

"What are they doing?"

"Phóng sanh—releasing living beings."

Phượng was puzzled, so the clown explained:

"Perhaps today is the full moon. The bird sellers trapped them days ago, caging them to sell to the wealthy. They buy them, release them, and think it's an act of merit."

Phượng laughed:

"But without them, who would catch the birds?"

"Exactly," said the clown. "They're clowns too, like me. Look, that woman's bargaining coin by coin."

Phượng watched a woman wearing a jet necklace, hair neatly tied.

"She didn't buy and walked on."

They followed her with their eyes. The woman haggled again at another stall, then finally bought about a dozen sparrows. Children crowded around to watch. As she prepared to open the cage to release the birds, the children lunged and grabbed them. Furious, the woman chased them, swinging her sandal and shouting. But the children were too many; they darted away laughing, each holding three or four sparrows. The woman clutched four birds tightly in her hand, still running and shouting. By the time the children vanished into the crowd, the birds were crushed dead in her fist. Angry, she flung them down, right next to an old beggar lying with eyes wide open.

With astonishing swiftness, the beggar snatched up the four dead sparrows and tucked them into his torn bag. The woman didn't notice or care. She left, still cursing. The beggar's eyes grew dull again, his hands trembling, his bandaged, bloody leg shifting as if in pain. Phượng wanted to hurry away, but the clown stopped her:

"That's a despicable old man."

"I think he's pitiful," Phượng said.

"It's his baseness that's pitiful. He lies there like a corpse, but in truth he's healthy and sound. One day I'll rip those filthy bandages off his leg."

"Suppose he is pretending—but isn't it pitiful enough to act so miserably?"

"You don't understand," the clown snapped. "He disgraces humanity. Why does he sprawl like a worthless turtle in the dirt? If he can't live, he should die, not stage such a vile show. Don't humiliate mankind."

"But don't you remember La Fontaine's fable of *Death and the Woodcutter*?"

"That's different! The man feared death but wasn't base. This old beggar, with his fake bandages and red dye, lying there to elicit pity—

he parades the vilest side of humanity in the open market. Look at him!"

At that moment, some latecomer women, unable to buy birds, wandered aimlessly. The beggar, sensing neglect, moaned and thrashed his limbs. When one woman approached, he cried and foamed at the mouth. She tossed coins into his torn hat and left. He foamed again.

The clown shouted:

"Hey, old man! What trick is that?"

The beggar fell silent and glared at him. Recognizing his rival—the clown who did handstands, swallowed ping-pong balls, and threw knives—he shut his eyes and played dead. But the clown wasn't done. He kicked the beggar's bandaged leg. The old man jerked up, shrieking:

"Oh people! He's beating me!"

The crowd stirred. Soon a circle gathered around them. The beggar wailed:

"He's hitting a cripple!"

"Crippled?!" The clown laughed, turning to the crowd. "He's no cripple. He's faking! Ladies and gentlemen, witness a duel between the clown and the beggar!"

Suddenly he tore off the bandages. The old man shook as if in convulsions. But the clown yanked him upright and grabbed his groin. Startled, the beggar leapt aside, quick and nimble—proof of skill. He squared off, glaring with hatred. The clown grinned:

"Come on, Lão Cái Bang, you attack first."

He struck first. The beggar parried and spun a swift kick, hitting the clown in the chest. Phượng panicked and dragged the clown away. The crowd roared with laughter and applause. The clown, in pain, fled with Phượng out of the market. She scolded:

"Why did you provoke him?"

"I didn't provoke him. I wanted him to become someone else."

Indeed, afterward the old beggar was never again seen writhing in the dirt. But the clown had to rest two days with chest pain. On the third day, he and Phượng performed again. This time the crowd was larger. Phượng stood with her back against a board, chest thrust forward, while the clown threw twelve sharp knives around her. The children clapped wildly. A balloon seller asked:

"You throw knives so well—why did you lose to that old man?"

The clown assumed the tone of a street hawker:

"Ladies and gentlemen, she asks why the clown throws knives so well yet lost to the old man. But the clown throws knives poorly."

The balloon seller asked the crowd:

"Do you think he throws well?"

"Very well! Very well!"

The clown said:

"No, not well at all. (He imitated a Chinese accent.) Me throw twelve knives, all miss. Not one hit the girl, right?"

The crowd laughed. Phượng was surprised by his answer. She freed herself from the knives, pulling them one by one from the board, while the clown turned his cap upside down and went around collecting tips. Then he did a little magic trick with an egg, and Phượng performed a card trick for the first time—quite successfully.

They made good money that day, so they decided to take the afternoon off.

They returned to their church corner at noon, packed their things, and went to a secluded shore with rocky caves to bathe. They dove for mussels clinging to the rocks and by afternoon had gathered thirty or forty. They roasted them over a small fire. Birds filled the golden sea sky, the sun blazing red as it sank. White birds wheeled over rippling waves, calling, swooping, drifting in the vast evening sky. Sea mist spread from the horizon. The birds vanished into it, then reappeared, wings glinting, diving into the quiet sea, rising again in thoughtful arcs. They turned black in the dusk, until they seemed only like falling leaves.

"Where do they sleep at night?" Phượng asked.

"In bird gardens—on an island, a meadow, or a swamp."

Phượng tossed more wood on the fire. The church bells rang for evening mass. She asked:

"Shall we go back to the church tonight?"

"Do you want to?"

"Let's sleep here, in the cave—it's flat."

The clown nodded, lit a cigarette.

"Where's the newspaper? I want to reread the news about the district chairman."

"It was smeared with food, so I threw it away. Today they reported how the district chairman ran off with that blind tycoon."

"Abroad?"

"No, just fled. The chairman took hundreds of taels of gold from the blind man to cover his business. When things collapsed, both were placed under house arrest, but they were allowed to escape."

"They'll end up fleeing overseas."

Phượng asked:

"And the publishing director and that writer—you knew them too?"

"Except for your father, all the others were old acquaintances. Back then they were steeped in politics, and even a decade after liberation they still were. Especially the publishing director—when Phạm Tuân orbited the earth, he was editor-in-chief of a paper. That news made him strut about, shouting at an older reporter who suggested not exaggerating it. He raged: 'Such thinking insults our national pride! An affront to our country's honor!'"

Phượng laughed, poking a burnt mussel from the fire. "And when you were a journalist, did you clash with him?"

"Many times. He liked imitating Lenin. In meetings everyone sat, but he paced the aisle, hands behind his back, head bowed, then suddenly pointed and spoke. Even the way he put his hand to his forehead while thinking—like Lenin. He would say: 'Comrades, endure hardships. Imagine, a Party secretary trekking to the Mekong Delta to buy rice for the people! What leader in the world cares so much? Only wood and stone would not be moved by such devotion...'

He went on and on. Finally I lost patience and cut in: 'You shouldn't orate so, comrade editor-in-chief. Because your eloquence rests on a false premise.' He turned pale, lip twitching: 'False? Where?' I said: 'Nowhere in the world does a leader go shopping for rice—that's for housewives. Why not simply let farmers farm and sell freely? Then people could buy rice like anywhere else. Don't ask me to be moved by the secretary's shopping trip. It's the collectivization system that makes peasants unwilling to work, causing shortages, forcing the secretary to buy rice. It's absurd.'"

The clown chuckled: "Now everyone sees that, but then he branded me reactionary. Today, after being dismissed, he has his three-step plan: first, refuse new assignments; second, return his Party card; third, form a new party to stir trouble."

Phượng asked:

"And the district chairman? What was he in the jungle?"

"A commune militia chief. My unit was in Long Khánh, a mixed-control zone. At night we ruled; by day villagers farmed, bringing tractors into our base area to grow beans and sugarcane. I befriended a seventeen-year-old village girl named Thu. Every morning she bought me Ruby cigarettes. I helped her weed beans, cut and carry cane. She was lovely, always smiling.

One day I caught a beautiful striped squirrel with a golden tail. The militia chief begged for it, but I refused—I meant it for Thu. The next day he saw it on her shoulder and grew angry. He warned me: 'That girl is suspicious. Don't associate with her.' I grew cautious, but she remained sweet.

Soon after, he ordered me and two guerrillas to execute the village headman, accused of betraying the revolution. I was the executioner. We ambushed him. At last he came, walking along the dyke. I leapt up. He panicked, fell to his knees, cowering. His hair was graying, his neck bony. He was like a cornered animal. My hand shook on the K54. I didn't want to kill him. But my finger squeezed the trigger. He fell. The squad leader dropped the written sentence on his corpse.

That night I had nightmares. In the morning, outside my hut, I found the squirrel cage tied with a white cloth—the squirrel I had given Thu. I never saw her again."

Phượng sighed. She stroked the clown's hair, coarse as roots, sun-bleached and unkempt. It gave her a wild, mournful feeling of fate, exile, and lonely desolation that seemed ancient as time. She wiped her tears and whispered:

"Lie down and sleep, my love."

The clown lay down obediently, hands behind his head, feet on a rock. The sea murmured, the sky was vast and star-filled. Phượng gently stroked his hair, feeling like a mother—like a mother cradling her son home from war, from hunger and bloodshed, rocking him until he shrank into a child again.

When the clown slept, Phượng began to sing. Her voice drifted in the wind, scattered among the rocks, fading into nothing, unheard by anyone.

14.

Last night the two of them did not sleep at the corner of the church; instead, they stayed in a shabby, unfamiliar room. It was a small gambling den, immersed in dim light, thick with cigarette smoke, the smell of people and liquor. Most of the gamblers were bus attendants, black-market traders, and some petty officials making side deals.

The clown joined in with great passion, having eaten nothing since the afternoon. Phượng bought a piece of bread to gnaw on alone and played half-heartedly just to support the clown. By midnight, his lucky streak began to flare up in the palm of his hand. His long, elegant fingers fanned out the cards, glittering like a peacock's tail. He played with inspiration, his face calm, without hesitation, without furrowing his brow or clutching his temples. He let each card fall lightly onto the mat like a drifting flower petal, yet luck kept rising with every hand. Crumpled bills of one thousand, two thousand, five thousand đồng piled up under his feet, scattered like trash.

By morning, the game was over, but he was not the first to leave the mat. He looked around the gambling den:

"Let's stop, shall we?"

No one objected. Some collapsed right where they were and slept, others stood and left. The clown tossed the bag of money to Phượng and said:

"I'd like to bathe in the sea for a bit, then we'll have breakfast."

But they swam no more than fifteen minutes, for they felt no excitement. Still, the sea revived them. The clown said:

"Let's find a really luxurious hotel."

They walked along the beach, climbed a rocky slope, and followed a small path into a hotel. They ate breakfast slowly, dully.

The clown studied the mother-of-pearl carvings on the lacquered folding screens that separated their table from the one inside. Four panels bore elaborate images of Mai, Lan, Trúc, and Cúc, though the lines were crude, cheap. The clown asked:

"Are you tired?"

"I'm not used to staying up all night like that. The food has no taste at all."

He said:

"Later we'll catch up on sleep, then go out tonight. I think there will be moonlight."

They were about to call for the bill when a voice from the other side of the screen said:

"The German Christian Democratic Party will win big. Already the Social Democrats have admitted defeat. The West Germans are throwing money around like mad—it's impossible to compete."

Another voice:

"The key is the Christian Democrats' program of action, and the West German chancellor's declaration on monetary unification. One East German Mark exchanged for one West German Mark—who wouldn't want that?"

The first voice commented:

"I think that's just empty promises. If they did that, West Germany would bear a terrible financial burden, hundreds of billions of Marks. They could fall into inflation easily."

The clown tapped Phượng's hand:

"Do you know who's sitting on the other side of that screen?"

"Captain Tùng. He must be looking for me."

The clown signaled her to be silent.

Beyond the screen the conversation continued, this time a strange voice:

"The failure of East Germany, in my opinion, was partly due to a leadership crisis. No one had enough experience to confront the West's schemes. The same in Czechoslovakia—they had to bring in a writer with no political background and make him president."

"But he is a wise and capable man. He lives in an ordinary apartment like everyone else, he goes out to farms and mines. I saw a film of him going deep into a coal mine, his face blackened like a kitchen god."

Captain Tùng's voice:

"But that's Haven in Czechoslovakia. Here we have plenty of writers... When the government is strong, they write poems and stories praising everything, even flattery of individuals. When the situation changes, those same writers churn out denunciations and criticisms. Like that writer friend of the Phi Mã car company director. He even wanted to go further."

"How so?"

"He issued some kind of seven-point declaration, typed and circulated secretly among artists. Everywhere you go, people whisper about it as if it's something extraordinary. But really it was just seven insults against the regime. Go to Chợ Cầu Muối or the Miền Đông bus station and you'll hear much sharper ones, far more biting, concise, witty, and surprising."

"So when the major invited him in, what did he say?"

Tùng's voice:

"At first he acted tough. He said the mission of a writer is this and that, responsibility before history... So I asked: And when you write melodramatic love stories, when you chop history into pieces for martial-arts novels, when you take crime reports from the police paper and paint them into novels—does that show responsibility before history? He fell silent."

A sigh:

"And what about the publishing director?"

"I haven't been ordered to question him yet. I only invited him to the office and played him a tape of a meeting between a former resistance fighter—let's call him X—himself, the writer, and doctor Z. He said: 'All our meetings are allowed under the constitution.' But three days later he fled."

On this side of the screen, Phượng said:

"Then maybe he's here to find the publishing director. After all, I'm not that important."

The clown:

"Let's wait. Hear what more they say."

But on the other side of the screen glasses clinked. Phượng peered through a crack. Captain Tùng and his associates wore stylish civilian clothes, well-groomed and fashionable. He looked more imposing than before, still very handsome. The two younger men with him looked fiercer but laughed and talked easily. One lit a cigarette and asked Tùng:

"Major, where is your 'never-to-be wife' now?"

Tùng said:

"That I must ask you. How did your surveillance go last night?"

"I went to the church corner but saw nothing. Looks like they've moved."

"Where to?"

"I'll answer tonight. I'm sure they're still lurking in this town."

"Did you go to the market this morning?"

"Yes. But they weren't performing today."

Tùng said:

"Then you should watch the gambling dens. I know that clown loves gambling. And the girl loves it too."

On this side of the screen:

"The war has reached us," the clown said.

Phượng stubbed out her cigarette:

"Let's get out of here!"

"No need to rush. Let's hear the rest."

Beyond the screen:

"But why are they all gathering in this town? The clown, Phượng, the publishing director, the blind tycoon, the district chairman... They could have gone to other cities."

Tùng said:

"Of course they could. But this is a coastal town, a hub for organizing escapes overseas. Criminals often take this route. My scouts have already photographed the district chairman and the blind tycoon here."

On this side of the screen, the clown said: "Good. Let them arrest the others first, then we'll leave. Now let's go back to our room."

They called the waiter, paid, and went upstairs. They shut the door and slept until evening, soundly, like children unaware of moon or sky. When they awoke, the moon had risen outside the window. Its light traced a long band across the tiled floor, broken across the mattress where Phượng lay dreamily.

"Still sleepy?" the clown asked.

"No. I just don't want to get up."

He stood at the window:

"Come here, the moon is beautiful."

But Phượng didn't move. She said:

"The moon is prettier from here. You come and look."

Indeed, from where she lay she could see the rocky shore. The moon looked like a mad girl, fluttering, playing among the waves and glittering rocks. The sea rippled gently, like rows of white flowers drifting from offshore, tender and dreamy, like children's laughter carried by the wind. The moon hid somewhere in nature, perhaps behind a rooftop or a line of casuarinas, perhaps diving in the sea itself, thin as a dragonfly's wing. Who knew where it was—but its light spread everywhere, glossy and soft like young grass.

The clown stood at the window, half his face in shadow. He played the harmonica with abandon. The small room echoed with lively music, mixing with the whistling wind and the sea's giggles. The melody was like a flock of white swallows chasing each other through the room, out the window and back in, circling over the girl's hair, the flowers in a glass, the mattress, the curtains, the mirrors. The harmonica's sound burned with excitement, beckoning, enticing...

Phượng sang as she walked, stopping by the window to look down at the rocks, up at the misty night sky, out at the shimmering sea.

Winter night, far from home, lost in mist and wind... She sang song after song, her voice stronger than ever, clear and fierce. *This evening mist is so poetic, the casuarinas droop their shadows on the shore...* She sang as if alone, without waiting for accompaniment. She shifted rhythms, altered melodies, paused and resumed—everything spontaneous, like clouds, like rain, like sunlight, like wind.

When the moon climbed over the casuarina forest, she stopped, as if someone had just appeared listening secretly. She laughed:

"Strange! Why on earth did I suddenly burst out singing like that?"

The clown, still in shadow, said:

"You sang in a trance. It was wonderful."

"I went crazy."

"I know you went crazy. But when you're crazy, you sing beautifully."

"That's because of your harmonica. And because you played hidden in the dark—like a demon pulling the sounds out of nowhere."

The moon now shone whole, solitary and cold, without a cloud, without a single star beside it. Alone it drifted in the invisible, whistling wind.

Phượng said:

"Let's go out. Do you want to come up to the rooftop with me?"

The clown tossed the harmonica onto the bed, took her hand, and opened the door. But as soon as the door swung open, they came face to face with a crowd of about ten people standing right outside.

"What's the matter?" the clown asked.

A young man answered:

"You sang so beautifully."

"Thank you," Phượng said. "Just singing for fun."

Another young man stepped closer to her:

"At first we thought you were playing a cassette tape. But after listening a while, we knew it wasn't. We bet on it, then peeked through the crack and saw you singing by the window, the moonlight filling the room—it was amazing. Each of us sneaked a look."

Phượng giggled and ran down the long narrow corridor. The clown lingered with the youths, shaking his head with a smile.

"She's having one of her crazy fits," he said, and quickly followed the girl.

15.

The next morning the two left the hotel for a small fishing village on the coast. It was a narrow, sheltered inlet, remote and windswept. The roads there were rough with jagged black sedimentary rocks. The winding slopes twisted through thorny shrubs and dogtail grass, while the remaining stretches were filthy black sand littered with shells, trash, seaweed, and rotting driftwood. The two mingled with a ragtag crowd of boat people from all over. They dressed half-rural, half-urban—shabby clothes, but cigarettes dangling from their mouths, golden-plated Rado and Citizen watches on their wrists. The hosts carried a rustic, benign look like the very earth and rocks, but their eyes were sharp as razors. There were wrinkled old women in patched blouses chewing betel, old men with checkered scarves smoking hand-rolled cigarettes, crouched on rough wooden planks. Three meals a day were laid out there: chicken, pork, wild meat. Empty beer cans rolled underfoot, cardboard boxes stuffed with chicken bones, wrappers from spring rolls and giò lụa. Guests sat in groups, eating and drinking crudely, worldly. They laughed, whispered, muttered, but in every eye there was furtive wariness, guarded suspicion.

The appearance of the clown and Phượng drew attention, for the two lacked the rough readiness of boat people. Not beggar, not street tough, yet not city either. The girl—young, wild, distracted, exhausted; the man—silent, foolish. They huddled in a corner of the house, eating discreetly, speaking discreetly, almost whispering. By late afternoon they strolled barefoot along the beach. She wore a flared dress, hair flowing loose; he carried a cloth bag. At midnight he lay in a hammock, playing the harmonica. The first night, no one said anything; the second night, people grumbled; the third night, a woman snatched the harmonica and threw it away. The clown was about to protest, but seeing her enormous breasts, massive buttocks, and above all her wobbling folds of fat, he shrank on his torn hammock.

"Sorry for disturbing everyone."

"Now you realize it? Why so slow, kid?"

"Because too much fat digests slowly."

"What? Are you insulting me?"

The woman raised her arm to slap him, but he caught her soft arm and gently let it go. She hissed and turned away, but the clown called after her:

"Hey, chị Hai! Did you lose something?"

She felt all over herself.

"Nothing's missing."

"Yes. But if you pick up my harmonica, I'll give it back."

"Ah! You stole something from me?"

"Just get the harmonica."

"No. Return it now or I'll scream."

"Go ahead. But if a third person knows what you lost, you'll be in real trouble."

She grew anxious, pressing:

"But what did you take?"

"Your bra."

The woman grabbed at her chest—indeed, empty.

"What? How did you...?" she gasped.

At that moment Phượng, lying on a mat beneath the hammock, turned and murmured:

"Don't bother wondering, chị Hai. Just fetch the harmonica bạck, or you might lose your panties next."

The woman, trembling, bent in the dark to grope for the harmonica.

*

The next morning the sea was rough. The sky was overcast, drizzling. The clown rose early, walking alone to the sea while Phượng still slept. Some boat people were awake, sipping tea at a long table, a small oil lamp flickering, knees hugged as they stared at the waves.

The clown descended the gravel slope. The drizzle didn't even wet his shirt, and he wandered aimlessly, dazed. The sea tilted, shook, growled, but offshore it was flat, blurred in mist and the horizon. Fine mist clung to his coarse hemp shirt, to his hair. He skirted the mountain's tip, clambered over high rocks and deep crevices, and dropped onto a clean sandy strip. The seabed bristled with sharp gravel. He walked farther to the distant headland; when he turned, all was hidden—behind cliffs, coconut trees, broad sea almond canopies. Everything seemed strange, vanished: Phượng, the old couple, those half-town, half-country guests. The oil lamps, the chatter, the meals, the suspicious eyes—like a dream of some far-off time. So illusory that if, turning back, all he found was an empty beach, he would not be surprised. Why were so many people, so many fates, so meaningless to him?

He looked at his feet: thin, black, scarred. Shin bones jutting like ridges between sharp ankles. Skin soaked, wrinkled, pale. Toes shriveled like stunted roots on rock. What nourishment was he sucking from this earth?

Last night he dreamed he was the last rag clinging to a scarecrow in a bare field. A whirlwind lifted it, caught on a dry branch, tore, then rose again, drifting among glaring clouds and dim sun. The dream ended at dawn when he opened his eyes to the stormy sea, gray foam, distant thunder rumbling long in the horizon.

He sat up and glimpsed Phượng curled up, sleeping like a winter animal. He turned away, wanting to leave quickly.

The horizon haunted him—the image of someone rowing alone out to sea, swallowed by the mist. The sky opened like a narrow door to devour him, then closed, clouds seamless again.

Soaked, he huddled in a cave like a small monkey. Time and again he had struggled to prove himself, to affirm some grandeur, but always nature's indifference prevailed—its fury, its splendor, its eternity. While he proved nothing but weakness, ephemerality—a shivering monkey in a dark cave. Hopeless. He wept. Foolishly.

*

By noon, when the sun was already high and the mist had completely vanished, Phượng went looking for the clown. The sea had grown less violent and warmer. She walked for a while, but the rocks and sharp shells made her lose her balance and nearly fall, so she decided to swim farther out around the cliff.

The coast was savage to the point of being barbaric. It was as cold as death, without the sound of a bird, of a beast, or a single flame.

At last she saw a dark shape on a small rocky point. When she was only five or six meters away, Phượng realized it was the clown. She called out, but he lay motionless, beside him a dead fire. Angry, she splashed water in his direction, but it was no use. Just then a huge wave crashed down. Phượng was swept away, her shoulder striking a submerged rock in sharp pain. She screamed, staggering.

The clown bolted upright.

"Help me!" she cried.

He spotted her immediately and shouted:

"Grab onto the rock! Don't swim anymore!"

But another wave struck. Phượng clutched her head; at once, the back of her hand burst into blood, torn open by shells. The clown leapt recklessly into the water, his feet gushing blood.

He dove down. The rocks were thick, covered with razor-sharp shells. His hands burned raw in the saltwater. Phượng clenched her teeth, clinging to those blades of knives, inching inward, her hair spilling loose, floating in the water like dark seaweed. The clown lunged forward and seized that tangle of hair.

When he finally got Phượng onto the rock ledge, she was exhausted, leaning against the cliff and crying.

"I'm sorry," the clown said softly, tossing dry sticks into the dead fire.

Phượng spread her hair out to dry. The wounds on her shoulders had nearly stopped bleeding, the pain fading in the warmth of the fire. The clown tossed empty shells into the sea, then roasted the ones that still had meat on the coals and handed them to her.

"These are clams."

"Where did you catch them?"

"In the rock crevices. What do you think of this cave?"

"It's beautiful."

The clown laughed.

"I was looking for a place to make a nest, so the phoenix can come lay eggs. If only you could lay some pretty little eggs, that would be perfect."

"Stop being crazy."

"I'm not crazy. I think laying eggs would be more civilized and cleaner than giving birth."

"Who would be foolish enough to lay eggs for you to eat?" Phượng retorted.

"Eat? No! We'd take turns incubating them. When they hatch into a brood of little ones running about calling, 'Mother! Mother!'—wouldn't that be wonderful? We'd have created a whole new race of humans."

Phượng was now roasting clams herself, eating alone. The clown said:

"Let's stay here a while, go back in the afternoon."

"I think they're watching us. They're afraid I'm police. They could send thugs to beat us."

"Then don't go back. Forget about them. I'll bring our things here later and we'll live here."

They lay stretched out on a flat rock. The clown felt peace in his heart, the sense of smallness, loneliness, and foolishness he'd had at dawn slowly melting away. He closed his eyes and drifted toward sleep. But Phượng couldn't sleep. She gathered the fire together to keep it alive. The surroundings were silent, desolate. The sea blurred with the horizon, the horizon stretched infinitely, and a sudden homesickness crept in. She was startled to realize she had been away nearly a year, drifting here and there like a dry leaf. The past returned faintly, fragmented, confused.

The clown lay on his back, eyes shut, gaunt, dark, and ugly. But she loved him, because he lived like a hidden collapse inside, a despair masked with a clown's grin. She knew only she understood him—his solitude, his terror, his eruptions.

Suddenly Phượng heard footsteps crunching on the sand.

A middle-aged man was leading a fellow in dark glasses toward the rock embankment. Both wore expensive but unkempt clothing. Phượng recognized the man in front as the district chairman, and though she didn't know the older man behind him, she guessed it was the blind tycoon. The district chairman carried a backpack. They walked slowly, chatting cordially. At the rocky ledge they stopped, the blind man afraid of stumbling. The chairman crouched down to carry him on his back, handing the backpack to the blind man. Perched awkwardly on his back, the blind man puffed on a cigar, golden-rimmed glasses tilted upward in a vacant way, but his mouth was not vacant at all—it grinned slyly, thin lips curled proudly.

Phượng woke the clown.

"The district chairman!"

The clown jumped up. Seeing familiar faces, he called out eagerly:

"Hey! Come over, brother!"

The chairman looked up, recognized the clown and Phượng, and set the blind man down.

"Why, Phượng! What are you doing here?"

"I came looking for you, uncle. Come up here!"

The chairman looked embarrassed, reluctant to carry the blind man again. He led him step by step. The blind man asked suspiciously:

"Who's that?"

"Phi Ma's daughter."

"Heavens!" the blind man cried. "Tell him at once!"

The chairman said nothing, just guided the blind man forward. When they reached the place, they spread out canned beer and cold food on the flat rock. The chairman lit a cigarette and tossed a pack toward the clown.

Phượng feigned innocence:

"Who are you with, uncle?"

"You don't know? My God, a very important man."

"Is he the tycoon...?"

"Yes, yes! And you must have read in the papers about my relationship with him."

"I haven't read the papers in a while. So you're the tycoon's son?"

"Son? I'm old already."

"Then what are you?"

The blind man threw a beer can onto the rocks and laughed loudly.

"A soldier. And I am the emperor! Didn't you see him carrying me on his back like we're roaming the world?"

The clown whispered to Phượng:

"He's old, why does he talk like a lunatic?"

"Because he's only half human, the other half an orangutan."

The clown stared in surprise at the tycoon.

Indeed, he looked like a monster: obese, round-faced, huge-bellied, thick-limbed, and completely blind.

"He always calls himself emperor," Phượng continued to whisper, while the blind man and the chairman spoke aside. "At home he has dozens of servants. He sits in the center, maids fanning him on both sides, another kneeling to wash his feet. When he stretches out his hand, someone immediately gives him a beer. After he drinks, he tosses the can into the darkness before him and someone always catches it. If he hears it hit the ground, he orders the servant beaten. His room has no lights at all, since light means nothing to him."

"But the servants need light, don't they?"

"No one is allowed in his room except his concubines. When he summons one, she must use a flashlight to enter. He identifies her by the sound of her footsteps, sometimes without even her voice."

The clown was delighted, feeling the same fascination as when he first saw a hippopotamus at the zoo. He called out:

"Hey! Emperor, did you bring your harem with you?"

The blind man laughed heartily:

"Wherever I am, there becomes a palace. How could I forget my beloved consorts?"

"But you don't need to choose beauties—after all, you can't see them."

"You're wrong," the blind man grew stern. "Do you think I cannot appreciate beauty? My ten fingers are my ten eyes."

"Then tell me—Phi Ma's daughter here, is she beautiful or ugly?"

"If I can't touch her, I won't answer. But her father and I are business partners. I've heard she's beautiful."

Surprised, Phượng asked:

"My father does business with you?"

"You know nothing? Haven't you read the papers?"

"I haven't lately. But as far as I know, my father has never done business with you."

The tycoon roared with laughter, drained his beer in one gulp, and flung the can hard into the darkness before him. This time it whizzed past the clown's ear—no one caught it—and it clattered down the rocks. But the tycoon's laughter continued:

"Poor girl. Phi Ma went bankrupt, and you don't even know?"

Phượng's eyes widened.

"Bankrupt? But my father is an honest businessman."

"Don't talk nonsense!" the blind man barked. "He was my underling—how could he survive when I've gone bankrupt?"

"I don't believe it!" Phượng shouted. "You're insane!"

The chairman raised his hand to calm her.

"Take it easy, child. You're too young to understand. Everything he says is true. Right now your father is looking for you. He'll come here sooner or later."

"But how does he know I'm here?"

"Whether he knows or not, he must be here by tomorrow afternoon at the latest. The morning after, we leave."

"That's not true!" Phượng cried, turning to the clown for help. "Don't use me as a joke!"

"It's up to you," the chairman replied. "If you don't want to know, I won't say more."

The blind man suddenly tilted back his head and laughed uproariously. Then he slammed a beer can on the rocks, snapped it open, and beer sprayed in a fountain.

"Return to court!" he ordered theatrically, springing to his feet. The chairman, pale-faced, grabbed his hand, but the blind man shook him off.
"I won't be led! Carry me!"

His massive hands seized the chairman's shoulders, pressed him down, and clambered onto his back. They staggered away along the rocks.

The clown said:

"We must leave this place, my dear."

"No," Phượng replied firmly. "I want to stay here and see my father, to know the truth."

"Your father will persuade you to go with him."

"I won't. But I need to know what's real. Do you believe what they just said?"

"Yes."

"Why?"
"Because life is a farce. I believed that long before I met your father, long before I even knew who you were."

*

The night was cold and dark. The sea was pitch black. The palace of the old tycoon was, in fact, nothing more than a shabby thatched hut hastily built under a mango tree. Unlike his habit when he was still the director of a company, the old man now allowed a small oil lamp to be lit in the hut. Beside him, there were only two people: his first wife—a large, pockmarked woman—and the district chairman. The blind old man lay on a jute hammock, his wife sat fanning him, while the district chairman sat pensively at the doorway, chain-smoking.

The blind man kept smiling. He asked the district chairman:

"Sad, eh? Don't you want to be my subordinate anymore?"

The district chairman sighed:

"Come on, go to sleep."

His wife also said:

"Go to sleep, dear. I'm fanning you here."

But the blind man still smiled:

"It's only evening, why sleep?"

"It's well past midnight already."

"Is it that late?" the old man asked. "Go outside so I can speak with the chairman alone."

The woman obediently stepped out.

The blind man reached into his chest and pulled out a wad of money. All in U.S. dollars of various denominations. He lifted each note to his nose to sniff, then pressed them to his cheek one by one. That was how he selected and counted money. Finally, he handed a few notes to the district chairman.

"Here's one thousand dollars. Keep it for yourself, in case we get separated on the way to the big ship."

The district chairman took the money, thanked him, but his voice was sad. The blind man asked again:

"What time is it?"

"Twelve forty-five."

"It's so late, why haven't our scouts returned yet? I wonder if they've run into old Phi Mã?"

"They probably have," said the district chairman.

The blind man closed his eyes for a moment, then said:

"Go call the writer, the publishing director, and the monk here for me."

The chairman stepped out of the hut, shone his flashlight across the mango grove, over an open patch of ground, and reached another hut. There too was a small oil lamp, a hammock, and a small table. He went inside and found the writer, the monk, and the publishing director sitting around a teapot, chatting.

"Has Phi Mã returned yet?" the writer asked.

The chairman shook his head, sat down next to the director, and poured himself a cup of tea.

"Nothing yet. But now the emperor invites you gentlemen to talk."

"Son of a b…" the publishing director muttered. "That bastard is getting crazier by the day. I think the syphilis virus has eaten its way into his brain."

The chairman said:

"But since we've already followed him, we'd better stick with him. Withdrawing now would be dangerous."

"I don't give a damn about him. Who needs him to get out? Plenty of people have managed without him."

The chairman:

"If that's what you think, then why are you down here?"

The writer:

"Come on, don't argue. Anyway, he's got money, ships, docks—his routes are safer than others. But what does he want with us now?"

"You'll find out soon enough," said the chairman.

He stood up, but the director pulled him back.

"Hey, chairman! Why don't you just carry him over here to talk with us?"

The chairman spat on the ground:

"Damn it, why be so polite? If you walk with ghosts, you'd better wear paper clothes."

"Who's walking with ghosts—you or me? Not only do you follow him, you gave birth to him. He's a blind orangutan, half-crazy, half-mad, yet you signed the decision making him director of the company. Wasn't it because you wanted to use him as a front? But he's no fool. He's an orangutan turned demon, trained for seven thousand years, already devoured ten Đường Tăng. That's why we're damned because of him, and hundreds of thousands of Saigonese are damned because they trusted him with their money. And now you have to carry him around like a servant."

The district chairman remained cold, staring out into the night.

"Enough babbling," he said. "If you don't want to go, no one's forcing you. Just like forming your political party—that was your idea, not his. He didn't urge you. You asked him for funding. You should be grateful to him."

The publishing director slammed his teacup down on the table.

"Shit!"

That was all he said before sitting back down.

The district chairman gave his final word:

"Whoever's coming, follow me!"

The writer and the monk got up. The three of them stepped out into the night. Along the way, they passed small groups of three or four people huddled under trees, whispering discussions, or drinking merrily around a low table.

The writer, impatient, asked:

"What's going on?"

"He wants to review your seven points."

"Really? Damn, I've forgotten them all. And what the hell does he need that for?"

The chairman laughed:

"He doesn't. That seven-point declaration of yours only amused the kids. The blind man needs only one point."

"What point?"

"The one right below a woman's navel."

"Bullshit!"

The monk burst out laughing. His hair had grown patchy, covering his once-bald head to about three centimeters. He patted the chairman's shoulder and asked:

"Come on, stop being secretive. What does the blind man want from us?"

"Nothing. I'm just taking you there to see how he counts dollars."

The writer and the monk glanced at each other, but it was too dark to see what flickered in the other's eyes.

They trudged on.

When they arrived, they found Phi Mã already sitting in the hut.

"Greetings, boss."

Phi Mã stood, shook hands with each of them, then asked the chairman:

"Where did you meet my daughter?"

"Out by the stone jetty."

"And where is she now?"

"Still out there, I think. With the clown."

"Did you ask why they came here?"

"No. But I'm sure it's not to escape by boat. They're just drifting vagabonds."

The blind man's voice cut through, silencing them all:

"Enough talk! Phi Mã, I went out of my way to have you found. Now you decide your daughter's fate."

"Of course they must go with me. Why else would I have been searching for them for a month?"

"You misunderstand me. Here's the thing: I don't want the clown to come. He's extremely insolent."

"The clown doesn't matter to me."

"But he matters very much to your daughter."

Phi Mã said:

"I will decide. For now, chairman, please take me to the rocky shore."

The chairman:

"It's two in the morning. We can't go."

"Why not?"

"The rocks are covered with barnacles. You can't walk there in the dark. And besides, it'll be dawn soon."

"What if they escape during the night?"

The blind man said:

"I've already set guards on them. Rest assured. Tomorrow we'll talk."

16.

"Go to sleep. Tomorrow we have much to do."

"I can't sleep," Phượng said. "I feel there's something strange about you. Ever since the blind man left, you've become distant. What are you thinking about?"

The clown listened to the sea and looked at the small flickering flame beside him. He turned to embrace the girl.

"Come now, sleep. It's very late."

"I'm not sleepy at all. It seems the tide is going out, isn't it?"

They looked toward the sea but saw only pitch blackness, though the sound of the waves seemed farther away.

"Tell me. What are you planning?"

"We're about to part ways."

"Why?"

"Because I want it that way."

"But I don't want to."

"You won't be able to resist your father's will."

Phượng buried her face in the clown's chest.

"You think I'll go with my father?"

"No. But I want you to leave."

"And you?"

"I'll remain a clown in this life."

"But I want to stay with you forever."

"You won't be able to endure me. We've lived together for just over a year. You won't last any longer than that."

Phượng showered kisses all over the clown's face. She said:

"No matter how we live, it doesn't matter to me, as long as I have you by my side. I need you, I love you so much. You know I love you deeply. I need a home, a family."

"But I don't."

"Don't what?"

"Don't need a home, a family."

Phượng froze. She asked:

"You're tired of me already?"

"No. I love you more than ever. But I don't want us to have a family. That's also why I want you to leave."

Phượng suddenly woke to the shock. She stood up. The flickering fire made her face shimmer in a ghostly way. She said in alarm:

"You don't want us to have children?"

"What for, to bring children into this world?"

"They'd be a source of joy, of comfort."

"But they'd have their own lives to struggle with—working, competing, envying, deceiving... just to carve out a place, and finally waving wooden swords in a park like puppets to stretch their lives for a few more years. Or, less fortunate, dragging themselves to the marketplace with a leg wrapped in bloodied bandages, feigning injury, crawling in garbage to beg for alms. The end is still the black earth, decay, worms, and oblivion. I don't want to play a part in that farce."

Phượng said:

"But your view goes against nature."

"Because I have only one chance to live in this world, and I want to live by my own way, not nature's. For there's one great, fundamental difference between me and nature: I have consciousness, nature does not. I know suffering, nature does not."

Phượng covered her face and wept.

"Stop reasoning. I love you. I can't be without you."

"I love you very much too," the clown said, "but I love freedom more. Since childhood I've lived a wild, wretched life. As a youth I was lost in school, among friends. I fought in the resistance and was also once a 'puppet soldier.' I've kept company with beggars, swindlers, district chairmen, monks, intellectuals… and none of that means more than a wildflower by the roadside. What more do I need, to keep going?"

Phượng said:

"But I'm not going anywhere."

"I know you will."

"Why?"

"Because the vagabond life we've lived for over a year is only a sport, a game, for you. For me, it is my entire life. I respect your freedom, so I must leave you. Get up and prepare. They'll be here soon."

"Who?"

"Your father."

But when dawn broke, the first to arrive was not Phi Mã, but Major Tùng, his pistol in hand.

"No need for weapons like that," the clown said. "There are plenty more here to arrest than us."

Tùng said:

"You're criminals too. Phượng is guilty of drug smuggling, and you're her accomplice."

"What about the others?" Phượng asked.

"I'll arrest them all" Tùng replied.

The clown flicked his cigarette butt down onto the rocks and said indifferently:

"You won't succeed. You're alone."

"Have you forgotten there's a border guard post here? But enough talk. Follow me."

Just then, the district chairman and Phi Mã arrived.

"Greetings, gentlemen," Tùng said, tucking his pistol into his windbreaker.

Both Phi Mã and the chairman stopped in surprise. The chairman said:

"Unexpected, but no matter, we'll talk later."

Phượng ran into her father's arms. Phi Mã wept, holding his daughter's head against his chest.

"I searched everywhere for you. Why did you run away?"

"I don't know" Phượng said through her tears. "Life made me weary. I caused so much trouble."

"I could have taken care of it for you. You never asked my counsel. Now promise you'll never leave me again."

Phượng sobbed.

Major Tùng said:

"Enough. Save your words for later. For now, all of you, follow me."

The chairman said:

"Tùng, I suppose you don't mind facing the blind man? He's your main target, isn't he?"

"Of course," Tùng replied. "I'm not afraid of him. I'm not alone here. I've already alerted the border guards."

"Then let's go," said the chairman, leaping onto a large rock ahead. Father and daughter Phi Mã, along with the clown, followed. Tùng came last.

They reached the village near nine in the morning. Since Tùng wore plain clothes, the people planning to escape by boat didn't notice him, assuming he was a captain or some new arrival.

The chairman led Phi Mã, his daughter, and the clown into a hut, then took Major Tùng to see the blind man.

A little later, attendants brought breakfast to the hut. Phi Mã rummaged in his bag for beer and cigarettes to set on the table. Phượng, seeing the worry on her father's face, asked timidly:

"The blind man said you were ruined, is it true?"

Her father said:

"Don't worry about that. What matters is that we've found each other."

"But it's important! How can I not care? I want to know how it came to this."

"I was drawn into a great gamble. Someone gave me money to play. I played. And in the end, I realized the money was stolen from our people. All I could do was run with him. You left before me—maybe that was for the best."

Phượng wept, clutching his shoulders:

"But I won't go anywhere."

"You must," Phi Mã frowned. "You're so young, far too young. This is just a passing madness of yours. You won't endure such a life, it's unnatural, alien to others."

"Yes, if I lived alone, I couldn't endure. But I have this man."

Phượng took the clown's hand and kissed it, smiling through tears.

Phi Mã turned to the clown:

"If you wish, I'll let you come with us."

"I won't," said the clown. "Nor will I stop Phượng if she wants to go. What you said is exactly my thought. Take her with you."

Phượng cried out:

"No! I won't go. How can you be so cruel to me?"

The clown sat in silence. All three were silent. Finally, Phi Mã laid a hand on the clown's shoulder and said:

"I advise you to come. What's there to cling to in this collapsing country? What do you expect from it?"

"I expect nothing" the clown replied calmly. "I expect nothing even from myself."

Phi Mã's eyes widened:

"Oh, you think of your life like that?"

"You think I'm lying?"

"No. You're not lying. But few in this world think as you do. So, you desire nothing from life?"

"I desire freedom."

"And what about your love for my daughter?"

The clown was silent.

Phi Mã sighed:

"With such bleak thoughts, that you still live, that itself is strange."

The clown suddenly laughed.

"Oh, that's why I became a clown."

He sprang up, pulled a red tomato nose from his pocket, fixed it to his face, bowed to Phi Mã, then held out his hand to Phượng:

"Come, let us begin our act: *The Fox and the Grapes."*

Phượng spread her arms in a ballet pose. The clown somersaulted twice in the air and landed before her. Phi Mã sighed and held his head in his hands.

*

Major Tùng swaggered into the hut with the district chairman. Hearing their footsteps, the blind man knew guests had arrived. He smiled and gestured for them to sit. He asked:

"You must be the Major?"

"I am," Tùng stood upright before the old man.

"You came alone?"

"Alone. But I've already informed the border guards."

The blind man chuckled:

"You told Quang, didn't you? Or Mãnh? Or Chín Thuận?"

"All three. They're ready."

"So am I. I've spoken with all three already. At dawn they came to consult me."

Tùng's face betrayed unease. He glanced at the chairman, who remained ice-cold. Tùng sat on a bench. He said:

"So what now? This village is effectively sealed off."

The blind man's face grew cold. He asked:

"Sealed off for what?"

"So none of you can escape."

"Escape for what? Who needs to escape, you, or me?"

Tùng raised his voice:

"Surely not me?"

The blind man laughed, motioning to the chairman to open beers for the guest.

"I don't believe you're so slow, Mr. Tùng."

"Ah... so that means..."

"It means that once you've entered our territory, you cannot return."

Tùng tried to sound cold:

"All I need is to fire one signal shot."

The district chairman patted the young officer's shoulder gently, like a father soothing a son, and said tenderly:

"No one will hear, little brother. They're all deaf now. Don't believe me? Fire ten rounds and see."

Then the chairman leaned forward slightly, pulled a pistol from his waistband, and handed it to Tùng.

Tùng recoiled, staring at the brand-new K.59, overwhelmed with dread. He froze, his face burning, mind dulled, not knowing how to react. The other two were silent. At last, Tùng regained composure:

"You're formidable. So, what do you want?"

The blind man said:

"That's what I want to ask you. I'll give you a code word to board the ship. Wouldn't that be easier than staying?"

Tùng felt his body collapse, ears ringing, vision spinning. He held his face, nearly trembling.

The chairman soothed him again:

"Tùng, you were once my soldier. I've always seen you as my younger brother. Listen to me. There's no other path. Resist, and you'll die here. Obey, and you'll gain much. I think, deep down, you still love Phượng. Phi Mã values you highly too. He has money in foreign banks. You'll escape, and you'll be his son-in-law—a rich man's son-in-law. What more could you want?"

17.

The ship arrived at noon, which surprised everyone. No one knew where it came from as it loomed into the waters, heading straight for the black sand beach.

People asked the organizers why there weren't any small boats to ferry passengers to the ship. They were told there was no need for small boats because the tide was rising; the ship would dock close to shore, and everyone only needed to wade out, climb aboard, and leave—openly, in broad daylight, without hiding from anyone, because the harbor had already been bought off.

But things didn't go as "smoothly" as expected.

To avoid running aground, the ship had to stop in waters about eight meters deep; it couldn't get closer, and because of that, trouble began right away.

Women and children were to board first, but most of them couldn't swim. Even though it was broad daylight and the sea was clear, those who couldn't swim were terrified once the water reached their chests. They could easily flounder if jostled or if even a small wave struck.

A rope ladder was thrown down from the ship, and those who could swim struggled to help the women and children aboard. The rest pushed and shoved each other, flailing in the water, kicking wildly, shouting and cursing. Children cried. Handbags fell into the sea, bobbing about, and the yelling was like a robbery scene. The ship's captain shouted from the bow:

"Damn it! What are you screaming for? The police will come and lock you all up!"

Handbags drifted aimlessly in the water.

The stronger men continued helping the women and children onto the ship. It took a full hour to sort out that chaotic mess. When the district chairman carried the blind man into the water, only then did Phi Mã suddenly realize something and looked around in alarm.

"Where's my daughter?" he asked, carrying a bag on his shoulder.

No one answered. He waded into the crowd, peering about.

"Phượng! Phượng!"

Still no sign. He walked along the beach, calling. Suddenly, he saw a man pushing through the crowd toward him. It was Major Tùng.

"Sir, where's Phượng?"

"I'm looking for her too. Just a moment ago she was right behind me."

"With whom?" Tùng asked.

"With the clown. He said he would escort Phượng to the ship."

"Do you think in the confusion they might have run away?"

At that, Phi Mã exclaimed:

"My God!"

"Come with me." Tùng urged.

They pushed through the crowd, wading back toward the shore. Tùng sprinted toward the rocky outcrop, leaving Phi Mã struggling to keep up, gasping for breath. Sure enough, ahead of them two figures were scrambling over the rocks hand in hand. With police training, Tùng quickly chose the shortest shortcut to intercept them. He leapt onto a high rock, then jumped down onto a flat boulder four meters below. Now he was right behind the fugitives.

He drew his pistol, about to fire a warning shot, but then realized it would panic both those boarding the ship and the border police at the post. So instead he shouted:

"Stop, or I'll shoot!"

He saw the clown pull Phượng down behind a rock, just enough time for Tùng to close in.

"Come out," Tùng said. "Your father's coming now, Phượng."

"To hell with you! Get lost!"

"No. I'm here on your father's orders. He wants you to go with him." Tùng slipped the pistol back into his pocket.

"I told you already. I'm not going! I've said so from the beginning!"

The clown stood guarding Phượng, saying:

"You're the police, how can you force someone to flee the country?"

"This is no time for arguments. I'm warning you: if you interfere, there'll be trouble."

At that moment, Phi Mã arrived, his face grim with anger. He lunged at the clown but restrained himself. Instead he barked:

"Step aside!"

But the clown didn't move. Phi Mã glared at him:

"What do you want?"

"I want to protect Phượng's freedom."

"Lies!" Tùng shouted. "You're just seducing her!"

Phượng stepped forward:

"Shut up! I don't want you meddling in my family's affairs."

Phi Mã reached to grab her wrist, but the clown blocked him. Tùng lunged forward, throwing a punch at the clown's face. The clown dodged and kicked at Tùng's leg but missed.

As the two fought, Phượng lifted her pleading eyes to her father. She saw how old he had grown: haggard and worn. He too stared intently at her. Then he stepped closer.

"Can you really abandon your father?"

Unable to meet his gaze, Phượng turned away, buried her head against the wet rock, and wept. Phi Mã stood behind her, placed a hand on her shoulder, and said:

"Come with me. Everything will pass. Time will erase it all."

Phượng only cried. Phi Mã spoke again:

"Now I have only you left in this world. And you have only me. Why shouldn't we be together?"

Phượng whispered:

"Everything you say is right. But I love him so much. And he loves me too."

"No, that's not true. If he loved you, he would go with you. I'd gladly let him come."

"You don't understand him. He seeks nothing. He'll never leave, Father."

Meanwhile, the clown was being beaten back. Tùng tried to push him away, turned toward Phi Mã, and shouted:

"Take her! Quick!"

He slammed a fist into the clown's stomach.

The clown grabbed his wrist, stepped back laughing:

"Your watch is gone!"

Startled, Tùng looked down, his Rado watch worth a million and a half đồng had vanished.

"You thief!"

But just as he was about to attack again, the clown tossed the watch back.

"Catch!"

As Tùng flailed to grab his precious watch, the clown dashed to Phượng.

The ship's engine roared; it began to move. The district chairman cupped his hands and shouted:

"Hurry! They won't wait!"

The captain bellowed from the deck:

"Damn it! Leave them behind!"

Those words struck Tùng's ears. The clown was almost at Phượng when Tùng drew his pistol, aimed at the sweat-soaked back, and fired.

Phượng screamed, rushing to the body that fell against the rocks. But Phi Mã's strong arms seized her. She thrashed, sobbing hysterically. Tùng swept her onto his shoulder and ran wildly across the jagged stones. Phi Mã ran after, not looking back at the clown.

The water rose to their waists, their chests. With difficulty, Phi Mã and Tùng managed to bring Phượng to the ship as it prepared to depart.

A rope ladder was dropped. Exhausted, Phượng hung limp, like a rag doll. Phi Mã boarded first. Tùng, clutching Phượng to his chest, held onto the ladder as others hauled them up.

The ship shuddered, then churned forward, prow turning toward the open sea.

*

When the clown regained consciousness, the ship was only a black speck on the horizon. The wound on his shoulder throbbed, swollen and burning.

He grimaced, staring out at the glittering sea; the ship was like a bird vanishing into the desert.

The drizzle from the previous day had left puddles in the hollows of the rocks. Around them, he found one of Phượng's embroidered shoes, a button, and something red bobbing in a rain puddle. He stepped closer. It was his clown's nose. He picked it up, fixed it on his face, then gathered the shoe and button in his hand.

Suddenly he saw his reflection shimmering in the rainwater: a wild head of hair with a bright red nose. He felt as if he hadn't seen that face in ages. It was dear, beloved, beautiful. He smiled at it, cheeks wrinkling just like on stage. Tossing the embroidered shoe in his left hand, he muttered: maybe he should dream up a new act with that shoe.

Early Rainy Season, 1990
ĐÀO HIẾU

Journalist G.Phương Thanh INTERVIEW WITH WRITER ĐÀO HIẾU ABOUT THE NOVEL *"THE CLOWN"*

G.PHƯƠNG THANH:

Hello, I've been waiting to hear about your "love story."

ĐÀO HIẾU:

Oh! It's not my love story, but that of *The Clown*. A love story that is neither romantic nor tragic. A love story between two characters who are, in some sense, strangers to society.

G.PHƯƠNG THANH:

Strangers in what way?

ĐÀO HIẾU:

A young lady named Phượng once decided to visit a poor village in a remote, desolate mangrove area.

She didn't go alone but accompanied a delegation of experts, led by a high-ranking official. The group entered a thatched hut that served as the commune office, but no one came to receive them. They only saw a peasant, about thirty, lying asleep on a bench.

G.PHƯƠNG THANH:

I can already feel the atmosphere building! It raises so many questions:

Who is this man? What is his background? And how would the high-ranking official react to such a sight?

ĐÀO HIẾU:

They woke him up. The Official told him to call the commune secretary. But he just sat still on the bench and replied: *"That's me."*

G.PHƯƠNG THANH:

Oh, that detail is marvelous!

A "cinematic twist": the whole delegation thought he was just a lazy farmer lounging about in the commune office.

That reply — *"That's me"* — so simple yet full of character, broke all protocol, leaving the delegation dumbfounded. And for Phượng, it may have been an unforgettable impression.

ĐÀO HIẾU:

After giving directions, the delegation followed the Official to visit the mangrove forest. Meanwhile, the commune secretary, fumbling around for his rubber sandals, didn't see them off. He simply stood under the thatched roof, watching the group slowly make their way down to the boat.

G.PHƯƠNG THANH:

I suppose that was the very moment Phượng began to notice him.

ĐÀO HIẾU:

Exactly. Looking out the porch, she saw the commune secretary leaning against the bamboo doorway, smoking. In the cool river breeze, Phượng suddenly saw in him a very lonely figure.

The commune secretary turned and met Phượng's gaze. They exchanged a few words. Phượng asked what he thought about the Official's plan to turn the mangrove area into an eco-tourism site. He replied: *"He seems so excited, it makes me uneasy."*

G.PHƯƠNG THANH:

That brief dialogue already reveals the spirit of the male character: indifferent, yet sharp and confident.

ĐÀO HIẾU:

Returning to the city, Phượng went back to her own world. For a long time she did not return to the village. She continued with parties, dancing — and sometimes went to the circus, because there was a clown who performed brilliantly.

G.PHƯƠNG THANH:

Another man enters the scene. It seems Phượng has a tendency to be drawn to unconventional people?

ĐÀO HIẾU:

After one performance, when Phượng gave flowers to the Clown, he slyly took her wristwatch without her noticing. Later she even praised him as a "genius."

One day, her father, Mr. Phi Mã, received news that she had been kidnapped for ransom. But it turned out only to be a prank by Phượng and her gang. However, this fraud led to an investigation linking Phượng to drugs.

Phượng got involved with drug smugglers not because she needed money (she was very rich) but because she was *"bored, with nothing to do"* and wanted thrills.

One night, driving her gang to make a delivery, she was tailed. Phượng abandoned the car and fled into a park, just as the circus ended. She rushed backstage and begged the Clown to take her away.

The Clown carried her on his motorbike down the highway, to a friend's house in a fruit garden in Long Khánh. They arrived at one in the morning and slept on a bamboo bed in the orchard.

At dawn, Phượng woke with a newfound sense of freedom. Wandering in the garden looking for the Clown, she saw a man approaching — it was the commune secretary. She asked: *"Why are you here?"* He replied that the previous night he had rescued a girl and brought her from Saigon.

It turned out the Clown was none other than the commune secretary she had once met. All this time, Phượng had only seen the painted mask of the Clown on stage, never his real face.

G.PHƯƠNG THANH:

Oh! That's an unexpected unmasking. And also the turning point that clarifies the love story of these two "strangers to society" you've been shaping.

And the Clown's portrait gradually emerges, clearer and clearer: sometimes a commune secretary, sometimes a clown, sometimes a twelve-year-old child stunned by death, sometimes a youth consumed by lust. Every story he tells shakes Phượng, as though she were, for the first time, confronting the raw truth of life.

ĐÀO HIẾU:

But the orchard was only a transit station. The Clown brought Phượng to a seaside town, his hometown, (where he met old friends, such as the monk Lu Zhishen). It was also a gathering point for boat people. There, new figures appeared — the District Chairman, the Writer, the Blind Director of a banking empire... all mingling between fiction and reality, creating a flavor of "social allegory": everywhere is a clown show, exposing the ridiculousness, deceit, and tragic dimension of human fate.

G.PHƯƠNG THANH:

I want to ask: did the Phượng–Clown couple intend to escape overseas?

ĐÀO HIẾU:

Why don't you ask them? Back then, they only came to town to perform. They performed in front of the market and slept in the cave at night.

"The Clown had nothing but a red cloth, a bowler hat made of cardboard, a small stick, a few ping pong balls, and a deck of cards.And yet, he could still draw a crowd.

For her first public performance, Phượng felt shy, but seeing how natural, cheerful, and quick-witted the Clown was, she grew more confident. She only helped with little tasks: handing him the stick, picking up a ball that had fallen to the ground, or lighting his cigarette.

But with her there, the Clown's act was less monotonous. She gave the audience a pause to catch their breath, and it gave Phượng time to gather the coins that had dropped on the ground.

The Clown would walk on his hands, upside down, so that his wide, baggy trouser legs slipped down, exposing his thin, pitiful shins. At the next show, Phượng thought to tie the pant legs with elastic bands, so he could stand on his hands more comfortably.

The audience laughed in delight.

But Phượng cried.

Because she understood the man called the Clown: a bewildered soul, lost in this world, unable to find the way home.

But then everything became ordinary again. By late afternoon, the two had earned a handful of small change and returned to their cave.

The Clown grilled mussels on glowing coals and handed them to Phượng.

"Where did you catch these?" she asked.

"In the rock crevices. What do you think of this cave?"

"It's beautiful."

The Clown laughed:

"I found this place to make a nest for the phoenix to lay her eggs. If only you could lay little eggs, that would be wonderful."

"Stop it, don't be crazy."

"I'm not crazy. I think laying eggs is more civilized and cleaner than giving birth."

Phượng said:

"Who would be foolish enough to lay eggs for you to eat?"

"Why eat them? We'd take turns incubating them, and when they hatched into a brood of children, wouldn't that be marvelous? They'd run about everywhere calling, "Mommy! Mommy!"

Wonderful! We would give birth to a new kind of human race."

The Clown lay on his back on the stone, eyes closed, skinny, dark, and ugly. But she loved that man, because he lived as a hidden collapse within himself, a despair wearing the painted face of a Clown. She knew that in this world, only she understood him - his solitude, his fear, and his bursts of eruption..." (Chapter 13)

G.PHƯƠNG THANH:

That excerpt portrays the Clown with the spirit of Alexis Zorba. Perhaps you've read Kazantzakis?

ĐÀO HIẾU:

Yes. And I've always wanted to create as many Zorbas as possible. A thousand and one Zorbas, perhaps. Each with a different story, a different character, but all "strangers" in life. Zorba lives explosively and urgently, as if he'll die tomorrow. The Clown too knows he may die tomorrow, but he lights a cigarette and watches as time carries him toward the abyss.

G.PHƯƠNG THANH:

That's the Clown after entering the underworld. But when he was still "commune secretary" he seemed ordinary, even dull. Why did you choose this sudden reversal?

ĐÀO HIẾU:

When Phượng first met the commune secretary in that poor, remote village, she sensed something unusual in his appearance, his way of handling the Official. At parting, Phượng asked: *"Why is someone like you here?"* The secretary did not answer — he himself didn't know why. And neither did the author...

In *L'Exile et le Royaume*, Camus sees the world as exile. Wasn't that poor village itself a place of exile?

G.PHƯƠNG THANH:

Very interesting. So, the secretary's "reappearance" as the Clown was not mere coincidence?

ĐÀO HIẾU:

Coincidence or not, the secretary would still become the Clown. He came into the world headfirst, feet in the air — already a joke. He became secretary, yet remained detached, bewildered before the very power he depended on — that too was a joke.

His shifts in social standing were not "up" or "down" but simply the inevitable drifting of a lost soul.

Though poorly educated and nearly anonymous, he was deeply experienced: and with experience came silence, surrendering himself to the drift of chance.

G.PHƯƠNG THANH:

So, one could say the Clown chose silence, instead of binding himself to any faith or ideal. Let me ask: in the novel, is that silence and surrender to chance meant as a philosophy of life you want to convey, or just the tragedy of one individual?

ĐÀO HIẾU:

It is the tragedy of mankind, not of one man alone. And he likes to let go, then watch what chance will do to him, where it will sweep him.

G.PHƯƠNG THANH:

You said it's a "tragedy of mankind," not just of an individual. So, in today's humanity, in which aspect of life — politics, society, or daily existence — is this tragedy most evident?

ĐÀO HIẾU:

It is an eternal tragedy. The tragedy of Sisyphus. The Clown too is a Sisyphus, straining to push his life up the mountain, only to watch it tumble back into the abyss.

G.PHƯƠNG THANH:

Yes, you compare the Clown to Sisyphus — the famous symbol in Camus' existential philosophy. But Camus ends *Le Mythe de Sisyphe* with a striking line: *"Il faut imaginer Sisyphe heureux"* (One must imagine Sisyphus happy). So, in your novel, is the Clown happy? Or just a weary, resigned Sisyphus?

ĐÀO HIẾU:

At the story's end, when Mr. Phi Mã (Phượng's father) asks him: *"What do you want?"* the Clown replies: *"Freedom."* Freedom is his happiness. He loves Phượng deeply, but he chooses Freedom — and lets her go.

G.PHƯƠNG THANH:

So, even in a world of absurdity and chance, the Clown holds on to one absolute value: Freedom. But tell me, is the freedom he chooses a positive one — to engage, to create, to shape his life — or only a "negative" freedom, to escape bonds, love, power, and society itself?

ĐÀO HIẾU:

There are many ways to embody freedom. The Clown preferred drifting. Stefan Zweig, Kawabata, or Renault Sarti chose suicide.

G.PHƯƠNG THANH:

I see. You mean freedom does not have only one path.

ĐÀO HIẾU:

Exactly. And existential attitudes too can take many forms. For instance, Rambert in *La Peste* chose engagement. But whatever form it takes, the essence of "existence" is one: it is rebellion. (*Je me révolte, donc je suis.*)

G.PHƯƠNG THANH:

Fascinating. So whether Rambert in *La Peste* chose engagement, or your Clown chose indifference, the core is still rebellion against human fate.

One more question: in your other works, do your characters also embody that rebellious attitude?

ĐÀO HIẾU:

In all my works (about 20 novels), each character has a different nature, fate, tragedy, or happiness. But always there lingers a sense of loneliness, estrangement from society. They cannot integrate.

G.PHƯƠNG THANH:

I see. So that sense of "non-belonging" seems like a thread running through all your novels. But let me ask deeper: do you see it as the private tragedy of each character, or a universal essence of modern humanity?

ĐÀO HIẾU:

Of course, in a work there are many characters with different thoughts and actions. But whether they chase wealth, power, or sexual passion... they cannot escape the human condition. That is the fate of Sisyphus. The only difference is they don't realize they are Sisyphus.

G.PHƯƠNG THANH:

Very interesting. So, in your view, characters may pursue worldly goals — money, power, sex — but ultimately they are just pushing their stones uphill endlessly. As a writer, when you write, do you want your characters to realize their Sisyphus fate, or do you let them remain unconscious, leaving readers to discover it?

ĐÀO HIẾU:

I want the readers to discover it themselves.

G.PHƯƠNG THANH:

I see. So instead of "lecturing" readers, you build ordinary details that plant in them a shock, a question about the human condition. That question is the spark of existential awareness. And it seems that is what made you a novelist, always writing about loneliness and estrangement?

ĐÀO HIẾU:

This is a delicate issue. Some might say I'm just following the "Western existentialist trend" expressed in Kierkegaard, Dostoevsky, Sartre, or Nietzsche. But if so, one could also say they were following the "Eastern existential trend" of Laozi, Zhuangzi, Bai Juyi, Li Bai, or Su Dongpo — geniuses who lived a thousand years earlier.

We can easily find existential thought in *Zhuangzi*, *Dao De Jing*, in *Book of Songs*, even in Nguyễn Du's *Thanh Hiên Anthology* or in *Chinh Phụ Ngâm Khúc*. And abundantly in Tang poetry.

.PHƯƠNG THANH:

What you say is fascinating. Indeed, not only the West has "existentialism." In the East, since Laozi and Zhuangzi there has been awareness of emptiness, of life as a fleeting dream. In Tang poetry, as with Li Bai, that sorrow merges with nature, becoming a vast loneliness...

So let me ask: when you wrote *The Clown* or your other novels, were you consciously continuing an "Eastern existential" line?

ĐÀO HIẾU:

I don't need to "continue" anything, but the characters appear as painful sketches of survival. I think if everyone felt that pain, there would be no wars. Humanity would love each other more. But may I ask you a question?

G.PHƯƠNG THANH:

Yes, please. What would you like to ask?

ĐÀO HIẾU:

As a reader, do you like the character "The Clown," and why?

G.PHƯƠNG THANH:

Very much so. Because he is unique.

He is not the usual "heroic" or intellectual figure, but a flawed, quiet, buffeted man. Yet within that silence lies a singular character. He chooses silence, but in that silence is deep experience, a profound awareness of life's essence.

I like him because he does not complain, does not try to prove anything, but simply stands there, with his painted clown face, blowing his short tune of life. And thus he becomes haunting.

In other words, he never intends to be a symbol, yet ends up as one — of solitude, of the longing for freedom, of the eternal Sisyphean tragedy.

ĐÀO HIẾU:

And what about Phượng?

G.PHƯƠNG THANH:

If the Clown is "the observer of loneliness," Phượng is "the one trying to escape it."

Her ability to recognize the Clown's uniqueness shows she is intelligent and sensitive. Phượng reminds me of female characters in modern literature: seductive, dangerous, and pitiable.

May I ask: after *The Clown*, is Phượng your favorite character?

ĐÀO HIẾU:

In this work there is a very minor character: the monk "Lu Zhishen," a friend of the Clown. I found him in my unconscious and pulled him out. I like him very much because he is as beautiful as a fossil. Did you notice this monk?

G.PHƯƠNG THANH:

Oh, of course. To me, he is a "priceless face," as you said - beautiful like a fossil. The monk "Lu Zhishen" - with his twelve wives - is clearly not a religious figure in the conventional sense. He carries a rebellious air, something unrestrained, wild, both worldly and transcendent.

Though he appears only briefly, he leaves a deep impression, for he embodies paradox: wearing monk's robes yet living licentiously - at once amusing and thought-provoking.

You calling him a "fossil" is apt. In the structure of the novel, he feels like a shard from some ancient time, surfacing suddenly, absurd yet weighty. He reminds us that in this chaotic world, nothing is absolutely pure; even religion can become another "clown show" of the human condition.

Though a minor character, he widens the novel's world, so it does not revolve solely around the Clown and Phượng but echoes with other voices, other paradoxes.

ĐÀO HIẾU:

My Lu Zhishen is also a supplement to the traits lacking in Shi Nai'an's monk.

G.PHƯƠNG THANH:

And how did you "supplement" him?

ĐÀO HIẾU:

Let me give you a passage — it will be more vivid.

"Right after the liberation, before returning to Duyen Hai, I had been chairman here. One night, coming back from a meeting, I passed through a cassava field and heard groans. I drew his pistol and crept through the dark rows of cassava toward the sound. It turned out to be a couple making love."

Phượng asked:

"Why did you interrupt their fun like that?"

"I didn't interrupt. At first I thought someone was injured, because right after the liberation the security situation was very complicated. When I realized it was just a couple, I laughed and asked: Do you need my help? I only said it as a joke. Unexpectedly, the man laughed and said: No, we're done. Aren't you the commune chairman? I've heard people say you're quite the player, and it seems they were right. I was surprised that someone caught red-handed could still respond so confidently. So I asked: Where are you from, friend? The man and woman had already dressed by then. The man struck a match to light his cigarette. The flare revealed a face full of beard and a bald head. His smile delighted me, it was confident, innocent, and oddly charming. I exclaimed: Oh, Master! I'd heard of you back in the jungle. Your reputation is well deserved.

And that's how we became close friends. Later, during drinking parties in the temple, the master confessed he had twelve wives, all of them nuns and temple women serving there."

Phượng said:

"He's too clever."

"Not clever. He was just doing charity for the world. I love such people." (Chapter 12)

G.PHƯƠNG THANH:

That addition makes the Clown and the monk more connected - forming a very unique "Eastern existential pair."

ĐÀO HIẾU:

Recently Martin Luther King said something I truly like: *"Even if I knew that tomorrow the world would go to pieces, I would still plant my apple tree."* I think that too is a kind of "rebellion" — a Zorba-like spirit.

G.PHƯƠNG THANH:

Many sources attribute this saying to Martin Luther King, but some documents suggest that it was more of an oral transmission than something found in his original writings. Even so, the saying remains much loved by many people.

September 14, 2025
G.PHƯƠNG THANH

ĐÀO HIẾU, Vietnamese writer, was born in Tây Sơn, Bình Định Province. He earned a bachelor's degree in literature from the Faculty of Letters, Saigon University.

His body of work spans multiple genres: novels, memoirs, short stories, essays, political treatises, literary criticism, poetry, and character memoirs, many of which have been published in both Vietnam and the United States.

He is also a well-known writer on social media.

Email: bukhutiensinh@gmail.com
Blog: daohieu.wordpress.com
Facebook: daohieuwriter

www.ingramcontent.com/pod-product-compliance
Lightning Source LLC
LaVergne TN
LVHW090400210926
848480LV00002B/407